# Demons
# of the
# Future

M.E. Clayton

# DEDICATION

For everyone that likes a man with tattoos.

# CONTENTS

# ACKNOWLEDGMENTS

The first acknowledgment will always be my husband. There aren't enough words to express my gratitude for having this man in my life. There is a little bit of him in every hero that I dream up, and I can't thank God enough for bringing him into my life.

Second, there's my family; my daughter, my son, my grandchildren, my sister, and my mother. Family is everything, and I have one of the best. They are truly the best cheerleaders I could ever ask for, and I never forget just how truly blessed I am to have them in my life.

Then, of course, there's Kamala. This woman is not only my beta and idea guinea pig, but she's also one of my closest friends. She's been with me from the beginning of this journey, and we're going to ride this thing to the end. Kam's the encouragement that sparked it all, folks.

Finally, I'd like to thank everyone who's purchased, read, reviewed, shared, and supported me and my writing. Thank you so much for helping make this dream a reality and a happy, fun one at that. I cannot say thank you enough.

# PROLOGUE

As I stared down at the two blondes sucking my dick, I wished that it were enough to get out of my head, but it wasn't. Though I could still appreciate their efforts, my mind was too consumed with a resentment that had only grown over the past year. I did not appreciate not being in control, and it was taking its toll on my disposition, though I'd never had a cheerful one to begin with.

Normally, the sight before me would be enough to make any man forget his troubles, and when these two had saddled up to me at Lullaby's, I'd been all in. However, they were turning out to be more *theatrical* than was necessary. I just needed them to offer up whichever hole that they were comfortable with, and nothing more. I didn't need the fake moans or false declarations of how they just *loved* to suck dick, seriously. Granted, there were some women out there that got off on swallowing cock, but I wasn't twelve-years-old with my first stiff dick, so I could recognize the difference between sucking dick because you really did enjoy it and sucking it because you wanted good reviews.

As it happened, the two blondes on my dick were just trying to stand out from the hundreds of other blondes that had come before them, but it wasn't working. Though Samara believed it rude when I called a woman *kukla*, she'd be surprised to know that I was actually being generous in calling them doll. I could easily call them idiots to their faces and not lose any sleep over it, so this was much nicer. Granted, Samara also knew that I only referred to women as *kukla* when I thought them empty-headed arm candy, but still.

Needing to get Nikel Ovchinnikov out of my head-*if only for a few hours*-I reached down, then tangled my fist in the taller blonde's hair, pulling her up while leaving the other one down at my knees to still pleasure me.

"What do you need, darlin'?" she asked as she ran her hands over my naked torso.

"I need you to sit on my face," I told her.

She squealed in delight as she eagerly climbed up on the bed. "Anything you want."

Little did she know that I'd had it all already. I'd grown up fast and hadn't ever really been young, so women had become a part of my life well before an age when they should have been. So, being thirty-five and a high-ranking member of the Russian Bratva, there wasn't much that wasn't on my sexual resumé. The only thing not on that impressive list was homosexuality or gender swapping, and I also wasn't into pissing or shitting on a woman, but that was about it. As for everything else, I was as openminded as a man could get when it came to the fairer sex, so these two weren't going to show me anything new, but they were more than welcomed to try.

As I stared at the second woman still on her knees, I said, "You, too." She pulled off my dick, then looked up at me for clarification. "I want to taste your cunt, too."

Her blue eyes flared with need as she stood up, and it was very possible to have two pussies sitting over my face while I got my fill. While my preferred kink was to make a woman come in public, eating pussy was in my top three, third to cumming on a woman. There was nothing like making a mess on a beautiful face, then fucking the girl while wearing the white ropes of cum everywhere.

"How are you going to fit both of us on your face?" the second blonde asked, her hand caressing my hard cock.

"Let me worry about that," I told her as my left hand reached up to hold one of her fake tits in my palm. While natural was always best, I gave two fucks if a woman was surgically enhanced or not. I was all for whatever made a woman feel good about herself, and if she needed fake tits, Botox, or liposuction to give her the confidence to live her best life, then so be it. After all, it wasn't like either of these sexy sluts were on the list to become my wife.

Not appreciating the extra attention that the second blonde was getting, the first blonde came up behind me, then wrapped her arms around my torso, her warm breath on my neck. "I love a good cock up my ass," she said, no shame whatsoever. "That big dick of yours should stretch me out nicely."

"Do you need prepping?" I asked, needing to know just how much of a professional she was. While it was remarkably easy to convince a woman to let me fuck her up the ass, there were those that I had to be gentle with, and then there were the ones that could take an impressive amount of anal abuse.

"No," she answered like I knew that she would. Her competitive side had come out, so even if she was lying, she wasn't going to let the other blonde know it. "I can take every inch."

*They always said that.*

Too bad they usually found out the hard way that they couldn't.

# CHAPTER 1

*Maksim ~*

It wasn't often that I frequented public places that didn't belong to us, but I was running on fumes, and so I'd decided to stop by Roasted to grab me another cup of coffee to get me through the rest of the day. Normally, I could go a couple of days without needing a pick me up, but I'd been busier than usual these days, still trying to find Nikel fucking Ovchinnikov.

It still blew my mind that I had a half-brother that was on a revenge kick to make me and my younger brother, Akim, pay for what our father had done to him and his mother. In truth, if Nikel Ovchinnikov had any sense at all, he'd be happy that Dimitri Barychev hadn't influenced his life. If we'd had the choice, Akim and I would have chosen different parents, Dimitr and Varya having been nothing but neglectful drug addicts that had failed us right at infancy.

Luckily for me, Avgust Kotov and I had become fast friends in grade school, so being the son of the Russian Bratva's Pakhan, Avgust had made sure that Akim and I hadn't ever starved growing up. While most people had given Avgust a wide berth, his connections hadn't scared me. I'd been resigned to not expecting a whole lot out of life, so I'd been used to violence on the street and all those other good things. My biggest concern had always been for Akim, and I had become more of his father than a brother early on, something that neither of us had minded.

At any rate, I'd been fifteen when both our parents had overdosed, and with little choice if I hadn't wanted my brother taken away by CPS, I'd gone to Mikhail Kotov, then had laid all my cards on the table, informing him that I'd do anything to protect my brother.

*I had ended up killing my first enemy at the age of sixteen.*

From then on, I'd done everything that'd been asked of me, and with my success rate, intelligence, and fearlessness, when Avgust had taken over as Pakhan for the Kotovs, I'd been selected as his sovietnik, both me and

3

Avgust becoming the youngest leaders of the bratva in Kotov history. There'd also been no objections to Avgust's chosen panel, which said a lot since he'd made the decision to appoint an entirely new hierarchy.

Though comparable to the Italians, we also had a ranking within the organization. Avgust was our Pakhan, which equaled an Italian Don, meaning that he was the head of everything. I was Avgust's councilor, which equaled that of an Italian consigliere. In Avgust's absence, I had the authority to make decisions for the bratva, but now that Avgust and Samara had a son, my job was to make sure that their firstborn learned how to make those sound business decisions for himself.

Now, there were three other men that rounded out the upper ranks, though neither of them was more important than the other. They were the board members while Avgust was the CEO, and I was...I supposed that I was Avgust's understudy for lack of a better word.

At any rate, Akim was Avgust's boyevik, meaning that he was in charge of the warriors, or torpedoes as we liked to call them. However, there were also the kryshas and bykis, which were our muscle and bodyguards. We had an assortment of them, Damir Ivanov being our deadliest killer within the organization.

Then there were Avgust's brothers, Bogdan and Melor Kotov. Bogdan was Avgust's obshchak, which just meant that he was the bookmaker of the group, and Melor was Avgust's avtoriyet, which meant that he had authority over most things if Avgust or I weren't available.

Apart from Avgust, I was also the only Vor within the higher ranks. Damir had also been honored with the title, and he was one of a handful that wore the markings of a Vor proudly. Where the Italians had Made-Men, the Russian Bratva had Vors, and it wasn't a title given to many. You had to prove your worth with a considerable amount of personal ability, intellect, leadership skills, and charisma. You also had to be fearless and relentless in a way that others could not be. You had to be able to walk down the dark streets with the devil and keep up, which I'd been excelling in since I'd been fifteen.

Now, while some people would believe that I'd been the one to bring Akim into the bratva's folds, that was untrue. I'd always done my best to take care of my brother and steer him towards a healthier path in life, but we'd been close enough that Akim had wanted to follow me wherever I'd gone, and while his rise to the top hadn't happened as quickly as mine, Mikhail had seen the intelligence in Akim and had used him accordingly.

That was another thing that felt like a bit of a kick in the teeth. Though Akim had always been a smart man, my IQ hit genius level, but instead of changing the world, I'd chosen to bathe it in blood because it was a lot more financially beneficial to be bad than it was to be good.

Now, twenty years later, I had more millions than I would ever need, and I had a job that I enjoyed to the detriment of my faith and any chance of making it into Heaven. Still, I wouldn't change a thing about my life. All the choices that I'd made had led to Akim being safe and well taken care of, and that's all that mattered to me. So, having a crazed half-brother seeking revenge on us was something that was bothering me down to my soul, and I wasn't handling it well.

"Daddy, I'm hungry," came a small voice from behind me. "Do you think I can get one of those muffins over there?"

"No," the father snapped. "I don't have enough money to buy myself a coffee and you a muffin, Mindy."

"Oh," she replied quickly. "Then…can you make me something to eat when we get home?"

"If your mom's home, she can make you something," the father told her. "If not, make some cereal."

"Okay," came her quiet reply.

Though a psychologist would have a field day with me as a patient, it didn't take my genius IQ to figure out why anger was licking down my spine at how this man was treating his child. Remembering exactly what it'd felt like to go to bed hungry, this man was lucky that I wasn't pulling out my gun and making his daughter an orphan.

When it was finally my turn up at the counter, I ordered a large black coffee, nothing fancy, then added two muffins, one of each flavor. This little girl was going to get fed if I had to buy the whole goddamn café to do it.

After I paid for my stuff, since my coffee was simple, the barista was able to hand me my drink and the muffins immediately. When I turned to get out of line, two customers back, I saw the non-descript asshole with his expensive iPhone in hand, the little girl looking down at the floor.

*I felt murderous.*

"Hey, what's your name?" I asked, doing my best to make my voice sound soothing and not like I smoked a carton of cigarettes a day.

The little girl looked up at me, her big brown eyes shining brightly, almost as if she was eager to make a new friend. "Mindy."

I held the bag towards her. "There are two muffins in here for you, Mindy. Enjoy them."

At that, her father finally pulled his attention away from his phone. "Hey, what are you doing?" he snapped. "Stay away from my daughter."

It wasn't until I turned to face him fully that he finally noticed my size and my tattoos. Though a lot of people in Port Townsend like to believe that the Kotovs, Sartoris, and O'Briens didn't exist, they knew damn well that we did.

His face paled a bit as his eyes widened, and knowing that he wasn't going to say anything, I looked back down at his daughter, then said, "Hey, Mindy…why don't you go right over there to the menu and pick yourself some dinner. Can you do that?"

She nodded eagerly, letting go of her father's hand without even asking him. "Can I pick anything?" she asked as she took the bag of muffins from my hand.

"Yes, anything," I assured her.

"Thank you!" she exclaimed before taking off towards the menu board.

The second that she was out of earshot, I grabbed her father by his arm, yanked him out of line, then pushed my gun up against his ribs as I walked us over towards the restrooms, though I made sure that I could still see Mindy from where we were.

Not giving him a chance to speak, I said, "I am Maksim Barychev. Have you heard of me?" He looked like he was going to piss his pants as he nodded. "Good. Now, here's what's going to happen," I continued as I took his phone from him with my other hand. "I am going to go through your phone and learn everything that I can about you. Then I'm going to assign someone from the bratva to become guardian to your daughter, and if I hear of you choosing to buy yourself a coffee over feeding her ever again, your child will become fatherless after I spend days making sure that you know what it feels like to be starved, abused, and mistreated." I pushed my gun deeper into his ribs. "Have I made myself clear?"

"Ye...yes...yes..." he stammered. "Yes..."

Letting go of him, I said, "Whenever you look at that little girl, you better give thanks to her. After all, she's the only reason that you're still breathing."

With that, I left the asshole to go pay for whatever the little girl wanted to order.

# CHAPTER 2

*Katja ~*

There were worst things in the world than being an IT specialist, and that was something that I needed to keep reminding myself of. I also had to remind myself that we all had bad days, and I couldn't let my one bad day dictate the rest of my week. If I did, then that one day could lead into one week that could lead into one month, and so forth, a trap that I had no desire to find myself in.

Besides, like most of the people on the planet, I needed my job. In fact, I actually needed two, but with my current contract having me on-call most of the time, I couldn't see another job being okay with that. Employers needed dependable workers, and though I was dependable, my current employment made it impossible to seek out a second means of income.

Plus, there were only twenty-four hours in a day, and it'd kill me if I couldn't visit my grandfather as regularly as I did now. Not only had he always been there for me, but he had helped raise me when I'd been a child, and being his only grandchild, we had spent a lot of time together. My grandfather had been the storyteller in my life, and the lessons that he'd taught me over the years were invaluable.

As for my parents, Ivan and Katerina Volkov, they'd been the best parents that a little girl could have ever asked for. They'd been attentive, loving, and both had the patience of a saint, never pushing me aside for something more important. Granted, I'd been their only child, so they hadn't had to divide their attention between more than one kid, but still. Every day of my childhood, I'd felt loved and wanted, and that was so important for a child.

I could also remember how I used to think that my parents had the coolest jobs ever. Together, they'd owned a Russian specialty shop, and they'd sold art, ceramics, toys, and whatever else that you could find in a novelty store. Plus, it'd all been from Russian culture, and whenever they'd get a new piece in, Dedushka Stepan would tell me the story behind it. As for Babushka

Anna, my grandmother had been a little bit more serious than my grandfather. While my grandfather had filled my head with incredible stories, my grandmother had instilled responsibility in me. I'd gotten the best of both worlds, and I knew how lucky I was to have had that kind of childhood.

Nevertheless, ten years ago, I'd been a twenty-three-year-old college graduate, ready to take on the world, never suspecting that my ideal life would be turned upside down with the robbery and murder of both my parents. They'd been doing inventory at the shop one night, and a dope fiend had broken in, shooting and killing them both, then robbing the place of what they could get cash for. It'd been senseless, traumatic, and crippling.

Unfortunately, things had only gotten worse when my grandmother had passed away from a heart attack only three months later. She'd lost her only daughter, and the heartbreak of it had been too much for her to bear. Especially, once it'd come to light that my parents had been in some serious debt. Unbeknownst to the rest of the family, the shop hadn't been doing that great for years, and when the dust had settled on my parents' graves, we'd lost everything.

So, after the death of my grandmother, I had ended up moving in with my grandfather, and I still lived in the house that he had loved my grandmother and raised my mother in. Now, while there were only a few years left on the mortgage, for the past ten years, I'd been working my ass off, using my degree to the best of my ability, and making sure that my grandfather wouldn't lose his house since he no longer had the help of my parents.

Now, as for the paternal side of my family, my father's parents hadn't approved of him moving to America to make a new life for himself, so as soon as he'd gotten on the plane, they had disowned him, and he had returned the favor ten-fold. In fact, I didn't even know the names of his parents or if he even had any siblings, and while I hadn't felt the absence as a child, I'd felt it when they had passed away. I could have used the extra support when they'd been killed, and more so when my grandmother had joined them in Heaven.

Still, even as dark as that time in my life had been, life had added to the heartbreak three years ago. My parents hadn't had me young, making them fifty-three when I'd lost them. So, ten years later, my grandfather was eighty-three, and three years ago, he'd taken a nasty fall, and I'd had no choice but to put him into an assisted-living home. While I had fought to keep him with me, he'd chosen to be pragmatic over the situation, and he had forced me to acknowledge that he needed more help than I was going to be able to give him with the crazy hours that I worked. It'd broken my heart, and if I was being completely honest, it still broke my heart to have him not living with me. Yeah, he was treated well and had friends, but it'd always been us, and I felt the absence like a hole in my heart.

Now, while my grandfather's social security helped a lot with his housing costs, the rest of his expenses fell on my shoulders, and life wasn't easy when you had only one income during a time when it took two to survive, never mind to actually enjoy life. By the time that all of my grandfather's bills were paid for and his monthly needs were met, I barely had enough to cover my own expenses and still be able to eat out once a week.

I opened one of my desk drawers, then grabbed the bottle of aspirin that I kept there. I knew that I shouldn't be complaining, but sometimes a girl just needed to purge all the negativity, or else become a viral clip of her losing her shit on some unsuspecting citizen. I did not want to become the person that had a mental breakdown at the gas station because the credit card machine was down.

*Yeah, no thanks.*

After taking two tablets, then washing them down with some room-temperature water, I cracked my neck, then stretched my shoulders, the hours of sitting taking their toll. Luckily, most of my job could be done remotely from my workstation, but there were times when I had to physically address a situation, and IT really was a thankless field. Nonetheless, I loved technology and the way that it was constantly evolving, and I was always ready to learn something new.

"These just came for you."

I turned at my co-worker's voice and saw that she was carrying a vase of pretty spring flowers. "What?"

Greta placed the vase on my desk, smiling down at me. "Secret admirer?"

I rolled my eyes at that.

*I wish.*

My love life was colder than a butcher shop, and if I had a secret admirer, then he was very good at staying a secret because I couldn't recall the last time that I'd been out on a date. Truth be told, if anyone was doing inventory, my life was rather sad when you thought about it.

"Nope," I answered, looking over the flowers for a card.

"That's a shame," Greta sighed. "We could use the excitement around here."

While I'd been working for the Tremaine Group for ten years, Greta had only started working here two years ago, so she was still optimistic about the place. Now, while I wasn't complaining about the company per se, Greta was going to learn eventually that our clients' demands were way more important than whatever we thought.

When I finally found the card hidden behind a stunning daisy, I plucked it from the holder, then opened it, wondering who in the hell would send me flowers of any kind. Though I got along with lots of people and even considered a couple of my co-workers as friends, it wasn't my birthday, work anniversary, or anything like that. There wasn't one thing in my life worth celebrating right now, so I wouldn't be surprised if it was just a simple mix-up with the names.

Pulling the card out of the little envelope, it simply read 'Thank you.

You're just what I needed', and my mind immediately began racing with the last few companies that I'd helped over the past week. It wasn't unheard of for a company to send us thank you cards or whatever, so it was quite possible that this was for helping someone avert a technological nightmare recently.

"What's it say?"

"It's just a thank you card," I answered, stuffing the card back into the envelope. "I guess someone out there appreciates us after all."

"In twenty years, when everything is technologically based, we're going to be superheroes," she predicted, her twenty-two-year-old dreams shining through.

I grinned. "Already designing your cape?"

"I designed it the day that I graduated with my degree," she quipped.

"Well, I'm not sure if I'll be up to all the fame, but we'll see in twenty-years," I teased back.

Greta smiled at me before turning to go about her business, and her departure had me turning back to the flowers. If they were a thank you from a recent client, then why not send cardstock with their company name or logo? Why send a random thank you that could be confused with any other number of clients that we dealt with? Plus, not that I was looking for handouts, but a lot of our clients were big corporate America, so why not add a gift card or something like that? It was usually customary *and* a write-off.

Shaking my head, I decided to forget about the damn flowers, then get back to work. After all, the electric company didn't take hugs as payment.

# CHAPTER 3

*Maksim ~*

We were at The Richmond, a table always reserved in the back for any bratva members, and though Avgust and I could take care of ourselves well, whenever we were together out in public, we always made sure that we had enough guards not to be caught unaware. Of course, if it ever came down to it, I'd give my life for Avgust, something that he knew as well as he knew his own name. Especially, now that he was married with a child.

Now, apart from the guards, it was just us, and so I didn't have to watch my tone or words as I would with an audience. Though I'd never purposely insult or challenge my Pakhan, Avgust and I were close enough that he allowed me to speak freely when it was just the two of us. It was also fortunate that Avgust's ego wasn't a fragile one, so there was little danger of it getting in the way. A lot of men let power go to their heads, but Avgust Kotov didn't lack confidence.

"I just don't understand how he's been able to evade us for this long," I said, the same thought that kept plaguing me for a year being repeated.

Last year, we'd learned that Akim and I had a half-brother that was out for some sort of revenge. While he'd been going by Klive Simpson and creating havoc for the O'Briens and Sartoris as well, Nero Sartori's genius hacker, Morocco Carrisi, had been able to finally get us a picture of him and a possible motive. We'd also learned that his real name was Nikel Ovchinnikov Barychev and that he was thirty-four, looked like both my brother and me, and was my father's love child from an affair that he'd been carrying on whenever he'd traveled back to Russia.

According to Morocco, he'd been seeing a woman named Arina Ovchinnikov that had lived in the same town as my grandparents, Esso Village. Arina had gotten pregnant with Nikel, and everything had been fine until the day that Nikel's older brother had fallen into a creek, drowning in front of Nikel and their close friend, Louie Manziel. Now, while Edik

11

Ovchinnikov's death had been ruled an accident, the tragedy had done a number on both Arina and Nikel.

At any rate, Arina had done her best to reach out to Demitri, but with no success, she'd fallen into a deep depression, and Nikel had been at a loss on how to help his mother. Consequently, Nikel had vowed to make our father pay, so after the death of his mother a few years ago, he had decided to come to the US to take his revenge on Demitri, something that I'd already suspected. Unfortunately for him, the reason that Demitri had never returned Arina's phone calls was because he'd already overdosed by that time. Now, while I wasn't sure if Demitri would have done the right thing by Arina, that was something that we were never going to know because Demitri had been dead by then.

Nevertheless, instead of taking that information and dealing with his grief reasonably, Nikel had decided to take his anger out on me and Akim, and after amassing a small group of thugs to wreak a bit of havoc on the town, his plan had been to start a war between the Irish, Italians, and us, but he had underestimated the way that organized crime worked in the state of Maryland. After five years of trying to get to me and Akim, he was the only one left, and with his picture and motives now known, it shouldn't be this hard to track him down, though that was proving false.

"The benefit to being a nomad is that you can change your appearance and name constantly," Avgust pointed out. "That phone call from Manziel's phone tipped him off, so it is quite possible that he went back to Russia."

"I doubt it."

Avgust grinned. "Me, too."

"If Akim wasn't in the picture, I would be handling this a lot better," I confessed as I eyed my best friend. "Anyone coming after my brother is a problem for me."

"Akim can take care of himself, Maksim," he reasoned. "You've taught him well."

Even though it was true, it didn't matter. I'd been taking care of Akim since the day that he'd been born, and that made him more than just a brother to me. He'd always been my responsibility, and I refused to fail him. Unlike me, he had a family, and if anyone should take the heat for Nikel's unhinged way of thinking, then it should be me.

"I'm also having trouble wrapping my mind around the entire situation," I admitted. "I understand that childhood trauma shapes us all differently, but it's frustrating to know that he is trying to get revenge for a skewed reality. Dimitri Barychev was a piece of shit dirtbag, and Nikel was better off without him." I leaned back in my chair. "I mean, I understand wanting to avenge his mother, if that is what this is. However, he really is a better person for not having had Dimitri in his life."

"You know, it is possible that he's hiding out in one of the other territories," Avgust posed. "The O'Briens and Sartoris wouldn't be looking for him the way that we are."

I shook my head as I reached for my glass of vodka. "The truth of the matter is that he could be anywhere. It truly is a waste to speculate on where he could be when he could be anywhere."

Eyeing me, Avgust said, "I could always put a couple of more men on your brother."

"And have Akim lose his shit?" I snorted.

Avgust grinned again. "It is important to allow a man to be a man."

Changing the subject, I asked, "How is Samara doing?"

"She is doing well," he answered. "Our son keeps her busy."

Through no fault of her own, Samara had been kidnapped by Louie Manziel last year, and he'd been a big enough bastard to torture her enough to leave a lasting impression. Thankfully, Samara had never been much of a wallflower, and so she had managed to get free and kill Manziel in the process. Avgust, Samara, and I had all gone to school together, so our history was a long one, and through a lot of trials and tribulations, she and Avgust were now married and working on their family.

After giving him an acknowledging nod, I said, "We'll need the ports for a last-minute shipment that's supposed to come in next month."

"Make the call to Provenza," he instructed. "As far as I know, the rates are the same."

"I hate being trapped in the middle of those two assholes," I remarked before taking another sip of my liquor, a comment that I made continuously.

"It is not ideal," Avgust agreed. "However, you have to admit that business has been better ever since Sartori got rid of Emil Schulz."

A few years ago, Emil Schulz made the mistake of going after Nero Sartori's wife, and to return the favor, Nero had wiped out the entire Schulz organization, giving us and the O'Briens pieces of their territory. Though divided up evenly, the Sartoris still controlled all the ports, and the O'Briens controlled the northern border and the airports. So, in order to benefit from either one, we had to pay a cut. Granted, things were a lot more civilized these days, but they were still the enemy at the end of it all.

Before I could say anything more, our waitress was back with a fresh round of drinks, and it was hard to miss the way that she was adding an extra bit of flair as she placed my new glass on the tabletop next to me.

"Mr. Barychev," she cooed, her low-cut top pulled down enough to see that she wasn't wearing a bra of any kind, which easily announced that her tits were fake. There was no way that breasts that large could be that perky if they'd been real.

Avgust let out a low chuckle, and I almost flipped him off. Once upon a time, he would have been in the same boat as me, but the man continuously made his devotion to his wife clear for anyone and everyone to see. If a woman made the mistake of hitting on him, he dealt with her harshly. In fact, it was to the point that most women didn't look at him longer than it was necessary to speak to him. Avgust had already lost Samara once in his life, so he was adamant about making sure that such a thing never happened again. To say that Avgust Kotov loved his wife was an understatement.

"Thank you," I replied simply.

"Is there anything else that I can get for you, sir?"

I tried to ignore the huge grin on Avgust's face as I answered the woman. "As far as my drinks are concerned, I am fine, *kukla.*"

"Good thing that my wife is not here," Avgust remarked evenly, knowing why I called certain women doll and why it bothered Samara.

Ignoring Avgust, the waitress asked, "What about anything else?"

Though sex wasn't my drug of choice, a blowjob always went a long way to relaxing a man, and I could definitely use some relaxing. "Meet me in the men's restroom in ten minutes," I instructed. "Be on your knees and ready, *kukla.*"

She grinned as if she'd just won the lottery before turning to see to her other tables. As soon as she was out of earshot, Avgust said, "And that is my cue."

"Not all of us can be married to the love of our life, Pakhan," I joked.

"Well, since you have never been in love before, that'd be kind of hard for you, no?"

This time, I was the one that grinned. "I like to live dangerously, but not that dangerously."

Standing, putting an end to our evening, Avgust said, "Akim will be fine, Maksim."

"He'd better be," I replied, needing it to be true.

# CHAPTER 4

*Katja ~*

I always had mixed emotions pulling my car into this particular parking lot, but there wasn't anything that I could do about that. As much as I wanted my grandfather at home with me, I didn't have the time or training to take care of him in the way that he deserved and needed. It also didn't matter what my mind knew, because my heart ached every single time that I pulled into the parking lot and drove off from it.

Granted, Windmill Gates was a spectacular place to live as far as assisted living went, but there was a very expensive price tag for the benefits of living here. Unlike lots of elderly residential homes, Windmill Gates didn't have a dorm setting, nor was it set up like a hospital. Instead, it was made up of a bunch of individual bungalows where certain residents were guaranteed privacy. Now, while there was a building that catered to specialized care and was set up like a hospital with a common room, if you were still an abled body, then you got to live in the bungalows, and you were checked on regularly. The bungalows also had panic buttons throughout the rooms, and they also came with two discrete cameras that faced the bathroom door and kitchenette area.

At any rate, my grandfather had been able to procure one of the bungalows, and though it was expensive as hell, it was worth it if it kept his integrity intact. Plus, his bungalow was equipped with support bars, and he never took walks alone. He hadn't fully recovered from his fall, and so someone was always with him if he wanted to hang out in the gardens or take a walk. The care was really worth the cost of admission, but I'd be lying if I'd said that it wasn't a strain. Nevertheless, I'd eat plain noodles for the rest of my life if it meant making sure that my grandfather had the best care possible.

Turning off the ignition, I got out of my car, clicked the key fob to lock it back up, then made my way through the iron gates to go visit the only family that I had left. At eighty-three, I could only pray that I had another ten years with him, then after that, I had no idea what I was going to do. While some people would accuse me of being co-dependent, I saw it as cherishing the only time that I had left with the man that had helped raise me.

Another good thing about Windmill Gates was their security. The entire place was gated, and you actually had to check in through a parking gate, and then after that, you had to check in at the lobby before you were allowed to enter the facility grounds. Again, all of this cost money, but it was worth it to keep your loved ones safe. There were so many nursing homes, assisted-living facilities, and elderly complexes that were absolutely horrible or run by greedy administrations that I was thankful to have my grandfather living here if he couldn't live with me.

Once I got past the lobby, I turned towards the left to where all the bungalows were located. The place had a serene feel to it, and if not for all the older people here, you could actually mistake this place for a vacation spot with how cute the bungalows were.

When I finally reached my grandfather's bungalow, I knocked, then waited patiently for him to answer. Since I knew his routine well, I knew that he'd just finished his walk after dinner, so the rest of the evening could be spent catching up with me fussing over him.

About a minute later, the door finally swung open, and emotion hit me hard in the chest like it always did when my grandfather opened the door, his welcoming smile lighting up his face. His eyes reminded me so much of my mother that it was a bittersweet experience each time that I saw him.

*"Beda,"* he greeted affectionately.

Though I didn't know much Russian, I knew that word like the back of my hand. "If I'm trouble, then it's because you made me that way," I teased before leaning in to give him a hug.

He chuckled good-naturedly. "Ah, I missed my girl."

Doing my best to keep the tears at bay, I pulled back, then looked up at him. "Not as much as I missed you."

Still smiling, he finally stepped back to let me inside, and as soon as he shut the door behind him, I took a seat on the small settee that he had in his living space, and because we were both predictable, he sat in the small rocker next to it. I also wasn't surprised that his place was neat and clean like always. My grandfather had become a minimalist after my grandmother had passed away, and I wasn't sure if that'd been because the memories were too painful, or if he was just trying to make my life easier once he was gone, too.

"So, what new things do you have to tell me since I saw you last?" he asked, and it warmed my heart how he was really interested. If my grandfather was my best friend, then I could only hope that I was his as well.

"I got some flowers yesterday," I answered.

His bushy brows shot upward. "A boyfriend?"

I laughed as I shook my head. "No. I think they're from a client that was just showing their appreciation for my help."

*"Dorogoy,* it is not good for a young girl to be alone so much," he chided kindly. "Don't you want a family of your own one day?"

"I'm perfectly happy with you," I teased, not wanting to discuss such a painful topic, something that he was aware of but refused to let me hide from it.

Once upon a time, I'd wanted a family. Though not a necessity for me to be happy, I'd dreamt of a husband and a couple of children as part of my future. Between my parents and grandparents, I believed in love, and I absolutely adored children. However, the knowledge that my children would grow up without grandparents or great-grandparents had ruined that picture for me. Now, while I wouldn't say that I was opposed to having a family of my own one day, I also wasn't actively looking to make that particular dream come true.

"You cannot let life frighten your dreams away, *dorogoy,"* he said. "If you do, then you are merely existing in this world, and you were made for so much more than that, Katja."

"I'm not interested in changing the world, *Dedushka,"* I told him. "I like my simple life. I like being able to do my job without interference. I like going home to a peaceful house. I like being able to have crackers for dinner if I want to."

His white brows furrowed. "You had better not be eating crackers for dinner," he scolded. "Your health is not something that you should toy with."

I grinned. "I am not eating crackers for dinner. I was just trying to prove a point."

"Bah," he huffed as he batted a hand my way. "You can prove it another way. Do not make me worry about you, *rebenok."*

"There's no need to worry about me," I assured him. "Besides, you've got better things to do than worry about me. How's your chess match going with Mr. Reasons?"

"He cheats," he automatically replied. "He's always tipping the board when he's about to lose."

"And how is Mrs. Turnbuckle's great-granddaughter doing?"

"She's just the sweetest thing on earth," he said, smiling fondly over the little girl. "If I could just teach her chess, then everything would be perfect."

"I'm sure it would," I chuckled in agreement. "What about you? How are you doing?"

He let out a deep sigh before saying, "I am getting old, Katja. While my days are still blessed by God, my bones ache and the memories in my head fade a little bit more each night."

Though a troublesome topic for me, my grandfather wasn't afraid to be honest with me. Growing up, he hadn't only told me stories with happily-ever-afters. He'd told me all kinds of stories, some wonderful, some tragic, some simple facts of life. He'd wanted to prepare me for the realities of life, though I'd ended up learning that lesson the hard way.

"You're as sharp as a tack," I argued. "You and I both know it."

He just smiled again. "Sharp enough to know that George Reason cheats at chess."

The rest of the evening was spent talking about the weather, sports, and a crazy television series that my grandfather had gotten hooked on last year. The topics were all mundane but safe. There were times when I could handle trips down memory lane with my grandfather, and other times when I couldn't, and he was astute enough to know when it was safe to touch on serious topics and when it wasn't.

Once it was time for him to go to bed, I kissed his cheek, said my goodbyes, then left him in peace. As usual, I began to miss him as soon as I started walking down the pathway that led back to the lobby, and luckily for me, the staff here was used to seeing family members crying all the time. So, I never felt embarrassed if someone caught me wiping away a tear or two.

When I finally got home, I immediately headed for the shower, hoping that I didn't get any emergency calls tonight. For whatever reason, I was feeling especially exhausted, and it was enough that I was willing to spend money on lunch tomorrow, rather than prep my lunch before going to bed like I usually did. I chuckled as I remembered assuring my grandfather that I didn't eat crackers for dinner, so I'd better not eat them for lunch either.

An hour later, I was crawling into bed, ready to put an end to this day, so that I could get started on tomorrow, and just as I was closing my eyes and getting comfortable, my mind wondered one last time about those damn flowers.

# CHAPTER 5

*Maksim ~*

I took a sip of gin as Akim let out a puff a smoke that I only allowed on rare occasions. Now, while I had nothing against marijuana morally, the smell was hell to get rid of sometimes. Luckily for Akim, we were in my backyard, and that was why I was allowing it. I did not smoke, neither cigarettes nor weed, though it sounded like I did whenever I spoke.

"I know what you're thinking, Maksim," he said after he exhaled. "I know what you're thinking, and I do not need an additional *byki.*"

Just like we all had specific titles for our positions, so did the other men in our organizations. Where the Italians had capos and soldiers, we had kryshas, torpedoes, and bykis. Kryshas were our muscles, torpedoes were our killers, and bykis were our bodyguards.

"I just do not like not knowing where the sonofabitch is, Akim," I told him, not bothering to deny it.

"While I feel the same way, we have other things that need our attention more than Klive Simpson or Nikel Ovchinnikov...or whatever he calls himself," he replied dismissively. "As far as I'm concerned, he is no different from any other enemy that the bratva have. We all know how to handle ourselves, or else Avgust never would have allowed us to join his family."

Though Akim wasn't necessarily lying, he was thinking like a man that hadn't ever had to raise a younger brother. He hadn't ever had to look out for someone else on a daily basis. He'd never had to worry about eating or trembling from the cold Maryland winters, because I'd been the one to go to bed hungry, so that he could eat. I'd been the one that had felt the cold deep in my bones, so that he could wear my jacket. Now, while I wouldn't say that Akim was spoiled or careless, his leadership and organizational skills had developed with maturity, whereas mine had been born out of necessity. Akim and I were not the same, and that made these talks a bit difficult at times.

Deciding to table Nikel Ovchinnikov for a moment, I asked, "How is

Mindy fairing?"

Akim grinned. "She appears happy enough."

After I'd left the café that day, I'd had Akim assign Karik Nikitin to Mindy and her family, and while Karik was more of a soldier than he was a guard, he'd still been a good choice for the role of Mindy's protector. Though we didn't have anyone on our payroll with the skills of Morocco Carrisi, Bogdan was still handy with a computer, so it wasn't hard for us to do standard background checks on people. Of course, we'd learned enough from Kyle Michaelson's phone that a full background check hadn't been needed, and with the help of all the information that we'd manage to get off his phone, it hadn't been that hard to prove to him that I'd been serious about his daughter.

At any rate, once we'd had enough on the Michaelson family, Karik had 'introduced' himself to Kyle Michaelson, and from what I understood, he'd made quite the impression on the young girl's father. Now, while Karik had other duties assigned to him within the organization, he made random appearances in Kyle Michaelson's life, and it appeared as if our influence was working in favor of the little girl.

"Does she?" I questioned as I shot him a look that he knew well.

After taking another puff of his joint, he said, "Two days ago, Kurik followed the entire family to the park. Kurik forced Michaelson to introduce him to his wife and daughter, and after joining Mindy on the playground for an hour, he feels as if the little girl trusts him enough that he can check on her at school now or away from the parents." Akim shrugged. "He'd like to question her away from her parents, so that he can stay on top of the truth."

Satisfied with that answer, I asked, "And how is Karina and the kids?"

Karina was my sister-in-law, though we were not close. She and Akim had met seven years ago while she'd been catering an event that he'd gone to, and according to him, it'd been love at first sight. He had asked her out, she'd said yes, and six months later, they'd gotten married. Now, while I liked her just fine, she was a bit shy and timid, and it was easier to avoid her than have to watch my tone around her.

As for my nephews, I had two, Alek and Gian, and they were six and three, and I saw them and spent time with them often. They were sweet kids, and they were going to be bratva one day, so it was easier to connect with them than it was their mother.

Nevertheless, Akim's family was my family, and they were another reason why I worried about my brother's cavalier attitude regarding Nikel Ovchinnikov. Where I had nothing to lose, Akim would leave behind a wife and children that needed him. Sure, they'd be taken care of financially should anything ever happen to him, but a wife needed her husband for more than just money, and children needed both their parents to teach them the ways of the world.

"They are well," he answered. "I have extra guards on Karina, and the boys do not go anywhere without one of us with them. They are even no longer allowed to visit Karina's parents at their home. If they want to see the boys, they must come see them at our house."

Perhaps Avgust had been correct, and I wasn't giving my brother enough credit. Though he had an army to help him protect and provide for his family, he was still responsible for them, and I was treating him as if he didn't understand the concept because I still saw him as the little boy that had depended on me for everything while we'd been growing up. Akim was a grown man with a family and a high-ranking member of the Russian Bratva, so maybe it was time to begin treating him as such.

"That is good," I remarked, feeling marginally better than I'd had before.

"You're letting our personal connection to Ovchinnikov get to you," he said. "He is no different than any other enemy that we've had to deal with in the past, Maksim."

"That is untrue," I argued. "This is the first time that someone has come after us for personal reasons. Everything before now has always been about business, nothing more."

"You know, for someone as intelligent as you are, you should know that everything is not so black and white in this world, *bratok,*" he chuckled.

The most frustrating thing about having an intelligence level as high as mine was that there were times when I expected the answers to come to me easily, and that was not always the case. For the most part, I didn't struggle with solutions, but when I did, I wasn't pleasant to be around. It was both a curse and a blessing, but given the choice, I'd rather be a frustrated genius than a *durak*. Especially, since I didn't have any patients for idiots.

Ignoring him, I said, "Just be careful. Do me that one favor."

Akim let out a deep breath, knowing that I was serious. "I am always careful, Maksim. You really have no need to worry about me."

"It's something that I've been doing since the day that you were born," I reminded him. "So, it's not anything that I see changing any time soon."

My brother grinned at me. "You need a wife."

"The fuck I do," I immediately retorted.

"It's time, Maksim," he said seriously. "You're thirty-five and-"

"And you have plenty of sons to carry on the Barychev last name," I pointed out, interrupting his nonsense. "I know that you and Karina have no plans on just stopping with two."

"A family would do you some good," he kept on, insisting that he knew what was best for me.

"I already have a family," I pointed out. "I have you, my nephews, and now Avgust and Samara are giving me more children to spend time with if I choose." I leaned back as I took another sip of my liquor. "I have a big enough family without adding to it."

"Fine," he relented. "However, I'm still not wrong."

Deciding to get back to more important issues, I asked, "What do we know about Mindy's mother?"

"She works as a cashier at one of those dollar stores, and she seems to be a hard worker," he answered. "Between them both, they can afford their bills, but luxuries are few and far between."

"Have Bogdan do a thorough background check on her, then we'll see about getting her a better paying job," I instructed. "That will tell us if she's with her husband because she loves him or if she just can't afford to leave him."

Akim gave me a quick nod. "I'll see to it right away."

"Also, have someone get in their home," I added.

"For what?"

"I want to see what Mindy has in the way of clothing," I explained. "Winter is already making an appearance, and I want to make sure that she has adequate clothing for the season."

"If she doesn't?"

"Then prepare Kurik, because he's about to go on a shopping spree with a little girl," I told him, making him laugh. "In fact, I want that house checked like we are CPS and doing a welfare check on the child."

Akim let out another laugh. "Christ, Maksim. Kyle Michaelson must have really left an impression on you."

"No, he did not," I corrected. "Mindy Michaelson did."

Children really were too pure for this world.

# CHAPTER 6

*Katja ~*

Luckily for me, Trevally's was known for its dinner crowd than its lunch rush. Since I wasn't a big three-course dinner kind of person, I made do with light dinners, though eating my fair share during lunch. If I needed energy, it was to get me through my day; I didn't need energy to sleep.

At any rate, Trevally's had a great club sandwich that was my usual go-to, and they had these seasoned fries that I'd stab someone in the eye for. Now, while I wasn't sure what all was included in the recipe, I was still pretty sure that crack was somewhere in there because their fries were addicting as hell. If I could afford to eat here more than twice a month, I would.

Anyway, the plan had been to enjoy my lunch in peace, then get back to the office at a reasonable time to knock out the rest of my day. However, that plan quickly ended when a shadow slid over the table before a man that I'd never seen before took a seat across from me.

Now, objectively speaking, he was very easy on the eyes. He had dark brown hair and matching brown eyes, and though he had a beard, it wasn't one of those nasty lumberjack beards. This one was neatly trimmed and looked clean; no danger of any critters making a home in it. His face had sharp features that gave him that chiseled look, and it all came together in a very appealing package. Nevertheless, his looks didn't make up for his complete rudeness.

"Excuse me, but...what are you doing?" I asked, not afraid of being direct.

"Katja Volkov," he said, making the hairs on the back of my neck stand up. "Thirty-three, works in technical support, is an only child...should I go on?"

Before I could ask him how he knew so much about me, he was sliding a small manilla envelope my way, and I didn't even have to open it to know that it was probably a background check on me. I mean, how else would he know

23

what he knew about me. No matter what, I was certain that I'd never seen this man before in my life. With as imposing as he was, I would have remembered.

Then he really shocked the hell out of me when he asked, "Did you get my flowers? A beautiful arrangement, no?"

Sitting up straight, my lunch forgotten, I asked, "Who are you?"

"My name is Klive Simpson-"

"You're lying," I said, interrupting him. "That is not your name. Your accent is clearly Russian."

He gave me a sly smirk, almost as if he was impressed. "For the time being, you will call me Klive."

"I'm not going to call you anything," I practically spat. "I'm leaving-"

"What would your grandfather think of your bad manners, *milaya devushka?*" he asked mockingly, and that question immediately had dread slithering down my spine.

Ignoring all the things that didn't matter, I got right to the point. "What do you want with me?"

"Before I tell you what I will be expecting of you, let me tell you that there isn't anything that I do not know about you, Ms. Volkov. I know where you work, live, and more importantly, where your grandfather lives, and even the number of that darling bungalow in which he resides," he said, and I could feel my blood run cold with his words. "Understand that I have done my homework thoroughly before approaching you, Ms. Volkov."

"What do you want?" I repeated through clenched teeth, infuriated that someone would dare threaten my grandfather.

He leaned back in his seat as he said, "I want you to seduce Maksim Barychev and find out what you can about the man."

My heart stopped in my chest as my eyes nearly popped out of their sockets. There wasn't a person in Port Townsend that didn't know who Maksim Barychev was, and if there was, then they were all under the age of ten. Everyone else in the city knew exactly who Maksim was, and only a fool or suicidal idiot would ever get involved with the man. He was Avgust Kotov's right-hand man, and they ran the Russian Bratva together.

"Have you lost your mind?" I hissed.

"No," he answered seriously, ignoring my incredulousness. "I am quite serious."

My mind was spinning with a million different questions, though it really was just spinning all on its own at this man's outrageous request. While I had no idea why he'd ask me to do such a thing, it didn't take a genius to realize how dangerous betraying Maksim Barychev was. Not to mention that I was the furthest thing that you could get from a spy.

"If you know anything about Maksim Barychev, then you'd know that he's not the type to be seduced by big tits," I bit out. "What on earth makes you think that I could pull off such a thing?"

"I've been watching Maksim for a very long time now," he answered, making my nerves fray with each word out of his mouth. "I am familiar with his type, and you are definitely his type."

Ignoring that, I asked, "How do you even know me? How...out of all the women in this town, why choose me?"

"A few weeks ago, I passed you as you were exiting your place of work, and I...I noticed you," he replied evenly. "There was something about you that caught my attention, and I thought that it would be the same for Maksim."

I set my palms flat on the table as I let out a deep breath. "Are you seriously telling me that you just happened to pass me one day, then came up with some insane plan to have me seduce Maksim freakin' Barychev to...to what, exactly? Play spy? Find out where he's buried a secret Kotov treasure?"

"For reasons that are none of your business, I need to find a way to get close to him, and what better way than to use you to do that?"

I let out a dark laugh. "You're asking me to risk my life by putting myself in the path of Maksim Barychev, but it's none of my business *why*? Are you serious right now?"

"I am not *asking* you, Ms. Volkov," he stated firmly, and I felt like I might throw up. "If you do not do as I've instructed, then your grandfather will not live to see next week."

Tears of rage immediately sprang to my eyes. "You can't do this."

"Oh, but I can," he replied coldly. "Perhaps he'll find himself in dire straits after his chess match with Mr. Reasons. Or maybe an accident will befall him after one of his visits with Mrs. Turnbuckle's great-granddaughter. Something unpleasant could happen during his walk after dinner, which would really be a shame, no?"

I could feel my entire body shaking, and my first thought was to call Windmill Gates, but what would I even tell them? Without any proof that my grandfather was in danger, I'd just sound like an unhinged lunatic. The same thing could be said if I went to the police. Of course, all my options were quickly cut off when Klive decided to go a little further with his intimidation.

"Yes, you can call Windmill Gates and the police to help you with this situation," he said, reading my mind. "After all, we are in America, and America allows you freedoms that other countries do not. However, do you know what is more revered here than freedom? Money, Ms. Volkov. Money has replaced Jesus as the ultimate God, so how many people do you think have sold their souls to me for bigger bank accounts?" He leaned his arms on the table, his brown eyes locking me in place. "All it would take is one phone call, Ms. Volkov. One quick phone call to end your grandfather's life. Unless, of course, you decide to do the selfless thing and get me the information that I need."

I was just as terrified as I was enraged, so it was hard to speak. Still, I managed to ask, "And what if it doesn't work?"

"You will make it work," he insisted. "If you want your grandfather to survive our new friendship, then you will become the best fuck that Maksim Barychev has ever had. You will be so good that the man will refuse to let you out of his bed. You will be so enchanting that he will keep you with him at all times, and that will allow you enough time to identify any weaknesses in his security."

"Maksim Barychev will kill me," I hissed, quickly brushing away my tears.

"Yes, he will," he agreed coldly. "But then, so will I, Ms. Volkov. Of course, *after* I kill your grandfather as well."

I couldn't stop the sneer that crossed my lips. "Because you think that Maksim won't find out about my grandfather?"

"That is a chance that you will have to take," he replied heartlessly. "You have until this Friday to decide."

"That's only two days away," I spat.

"Yes, it is. So, I guess you better decide quickly."

Before I could say anything more, he stood up, then walked out of the restaurant like he hadn't just upended my entire life in less than fifteen minutes, and I was left with a fear that threatened to make me pass out. Suddenly, everyone was the enemy, and I had no idea how to keep my grandfather safe from whatever this was.

With shaky fingers, I finally opened the envelope that he'd left on the table, and when picture after picture of my grandfather spilled out, it was all that I could do not to fall apart.

# CHAPTER 7

*Maksim ~*

While Karik had left some time ago, I had decided to stick around and have a few drinks. By his accounts, Kyle Michaelson had seen the light, and Mindy was being well taken care of. Of course, that didn't mean that I was going to pull his detail, but I felt better about the little girl. Right now, all that was left was to get Mindy's mother a better job, and then we'd see where things would go from there.

At any rate, when I had decided to stick around and just relax for a moment, I hadn't expected *her* to walk through the front doors of The Swan. Now, while the scenery in here was always that of beautiful and built women, it hadn't been her face or body that had caught my eye. Truth be told, a beautiful face could be achieved with the right makeup, and a perfect body could be achieved with a great plastic surgeon, so neither achievement was impressive to me, though I could appreciate the effort.

Anyway, it'd been her eyes that had drawn me in, and I was curious to know if the color was real or if she wore contacts. Even from where I was sitting, when she had looked up at the waitress to order her drink, I could see how bright her yellow orbs had been. They looked like liquid gold, and if they were real, then that was a miracle in itself. Many women did their makeup to give them that doll-eyed look, and now I could understand why.

From where I'd been observing her, without the heels, she looked to be around five-foot-three, and that frame of hers was overflowing with curves upon curves. She was wearing a dark grey dress that fell just above her knees, and I liked that. I liked how she'd chosen classy over obvious, because there was just something about unwrapping gifts. Her black heels also matched her black purse and the black strands of silk that were hanging loosely down to the middle of her back. While The Swan wasn't exactly classy, it also wasn't a dive bar; it was something in between.

As I stared at her, I realized that I wasn't everyone's type, and it was very possible that she was waiting for someone, though if she was, that man was a fool to allow her out of his sight. The woman was breathtakingly beautiful, and any man that let her run around freely didn't deserve her. Of course, as she pulled out her phone, then fired off a message, she could also be meeting a friend of hers.

Still, as I'd been deciding whether I should approach her or not, I notice one of the men from the bar make his way over to her table, and when he immediately sat down, I no longer cared if she was waiting for someone or not. If she was going to go home with anyone tonight, it was going to be me.

Grabbing my drink, I stood up, then walked over to the table, and as soon as they both noticed me, I slid my eyes to the left, then told the man, "I can see that you are lost. Would you like my help finding your way back to the bar?"

As predicted, his face lost all color as he began stammering, knowing exactly who I was. "Uh...yeah, no...I know my way...thanks."

The second that he vacated his seat, I sat down, and the beauty sitting across from me just stared at me, and with her face giving nothing away, I wasn't sure if she was impressed or horrified. Of course, as soon as I introduced myself, I'd find out.

"Do you do that often?" she asked, her voice sounding like sex slithering down a stripper pole.

"No," I answered honestly. "However, I saw you first."

She arched a brow as her head reared back a bit. "Like a little boy that doesn't like sharing his toys?"

I set my glass on the table. "More like a grown man that knows what he wants."

Her amber-colored eyes slid over my face, then down to my chest, and though I was wearing a jacket that covered everything, there was still no mistaking all the tattoos that were visible outside the neckline of my shirt. If I wasn't her type, then that would be a shame. Nevertheless, I was secure enough in my manhood to not take rejection personally.

"What is your name?" I finally asked.

"Katja," she answered, and though she had no Russian accent to speak of, her name gave away her heritage clearly enough.

"And what is your last name, Katja?"

"Volkov," she answered, proving further that she was of Russian descent.

"I am Maksim Barychev," I told her, and a bit of apprehension flashed in those golden orbs of hers.

"Yes, I know," she answered, surprising me a bit.

My eyes narrowed. "And how do you know?"

"I've lived in Port Townsend all my life," she answered. "It's kind of hard to live here and not know who you are. The Kotovs as well."

While her answer was valid, something was off. Though my reputation was legendary, my face wasn't as popular as you'd think. I didn't mingle with the population of Port Townsend much, and whenever I was out and about, it was usually during the cover of night. For the most part, I only associated with my bratva brothers, so even if she'd heard of me, recognizing my face was something entirely different. Plus, who did she know that would point me out to her? Because I knew for a fact that I'd never seen this woman in all my thirty-five years; it would be impossible to forget her eyes.

Trusting my instincts, I asked, "What brings you to The Swan tonight, Katja?"

"I was supposed to meet my friend here to celebrate her promotion at work, but she just texted me that she has to cancel," she lied.

Staring at her, not only was my intelligence above average, but I also knew how to read people, and Katja Volkov was lying to me. Now that I knew that something was off, all the signs were there. Her body language was giving her away, and had I not been so enraptured with those damn eyes of hers, then I would have noticed her nervousness sooner.

"That's a shame," I remarked evenly as I leaned back in the seat, grabbing my glass to take another drink of the clear liquid.

Before she could say anything, the waitress was back with a single glass of red wine, and that just had me more suspicious. A celebration that required wine would not take place in an establishment like The Swan. If what she'd said was true, then they would have chosen someplace that would have resembled a restaurant more than a bar.

When Katja reached for her purse, I said, "Whatever she wants, put it on my tab."

Catarina gave me a quick nod. "Of course, Mr. Barychev."

Katja quickly objected. "Oh, no. That's not necessary."

"Catarina," I said, effectively dismissing her.

"Uh...thank you," Katja muttered, and I noticed how her hands shook a little as she put her wallet back in her purse.

*Interesting.*

"Not a problem," I replied smoothly. "As archaic as it seems in this progressive world of ours, I still believe in men still opening doors, paying for dinner, and everything else that used to be seen as simple manners."

Her eyes shifted a bit before she said, "While you may have a point, allowing a stranger to pay for my drink could also send a wrong message, and a woman can never be too careful."

I leaned my arms on the table. "Unlike most men, I don't place the value of a woman's company at the same price as a glass of wine, Katja," I told her. "If I am going to pay for pussy, then I would hope that the woman would possess enough self-respect to charge me more than the price of a drink."

Katja's cheeks immediately turned pink, but she didn't cower. "Do you pay for sex often?"

"I have never paid for sex," I informed her. "Whatever money that has exchanged hands, it was to pay for the peace and quiet afterwards." I leaned back in my seat. "Men do not pay for sex, *lyublyu*. They pay for the uncomplicated departure afterwards."

Her fingers started to fiddle around the stem of her wineglass as her eyes started to dart around again, and I'd give my fortune to know what she was really thinking. She was obviously nervous, but she wasn't getting up to leave or asking me to leave, so it had me wondering what her agenda was. At this point, I had no idea if she was attracted to me or not, but whatever had her still seated in her chair was intriguing me more and more.

Suddenly, those brilliant eyes of hers looked my way. "Would you excuse me a second?" she asked politely. "I'd...I just need to go freshen up a little."

Since she'd just gotten here, she didn't need to freshen up, so this was obviously an attempt to escape the uncomfortable turn that our conversation had just taken, or else she was going to go to the restroom to give her some time to come up with an excuse as to why she was going to have to leave.

"Of course," I agreed easily, already knowing that I was going to shoot Bogdan a text to do a background check on her as soon as she headed towards the restrooms.

Giving me a tentative smile, she grabbed her purse, stood up, then headed towards the back. What she didn't know was that she only had five minutes before I was going to make my way back there to see just what in the fuck she was about.

# CHAPTER 8

*Katja ~*

I felt like my heart was going to beat clean out of my chest. As soon as the restroom door shut behind me, my nerves ran free, and I could feel myself shaking everywhere. I was toying with the Russian Bratva, and I could see the lights of the freight train heading straight for me.

After Klive had left me with all the proof of how he could ruin my life, I'd taken the envelope back to the office with me, but I hadn't looked thoroughly through it until I'd gotten home that night. Of course, as soon as I'd gotten off work, I'd gone straight to Windmill Gates to check on my grandfather, and I'd never felt so relieved and so panicked at the same time.

It hadn't been until I'd gotten home and locked the front door behind me that I had opened the contents of the envelope, then had gone through every picture and piece of paper. As suspected, Klive had done a thorough background check on me, and while I had no idea how he'd gotten so much information on me, he'd had, and that wasn't the only thing. To my surprise, he had also included a picture of Maksim Barychev, but that picture hadn't done the man justice.

Armed with knowing what he looked like, I'd known that it was him the second that he had walked up to the table, and I hadn't been prepared for just how big the man was. He easily stood at around six-foot-four, and he had dark brown hair that looked like the smoothest chocolate, plus matching brown eyes that looked like demons resided in them. Most men with brown eyes had that hooded bedroom look about them, but not Maksim Barychev. His dark eyes were sharp, cold, and intelligent. Nevertheless, there was no denying that he had to be one of the most gorgeous men that I'd ever seen.

Then there was that body of his. Even with a jacket on, you could tell that he was ripped from head to damn toe. If there was even an ounce of fat on him, I'd sell my soul to Satan himself. Plus, if that weren't enough, the man had enough tattoos to make a woman drool, and the way that they peeked out of his shirt collar was sexy as hell. For all that he was a ruthless killer, it was easy to fall under the spell of his looks. Never mind that his voice sounded like it was made for sin. It was low, raspy, and sounded like someone might have stepped on his larynx at some point.

At any rate, it'd only taken five minutes in his company to recognize that I was way in over my head. I had no idea what to do, and the reflection in the mirror above the sink had no answers for me. Klive had made a good point about how Maksim may kill only me, but how he would kill *both* me and my grandfather, so the choice was an easy one, though the execution harder than I'd expected.

There was also the fact that I hadn't even had time to prepare myself for tonight. When Klive had called me from an unknown number earlier today for my answer, I hadn't expected a second call from him so soon. However, that's exactly what had happened when he'd called to tell me that Maksim was at The Swan, and that I'd better hurry and make something happen. I hadn't even had time to ask him how he'd known where Maksim had been, but if Klive had no problem spying on me, then I could see him stalking Maksim for whatever reason.

At any rate, my nerves were practically fried, and I had no idea how I was going to pull this off. As I thought about running, there was no guarantee that Klive wasn't watching from a dark hole somewhere, waiting to see if I was actually going through with my promise to help him. It also didn't help that I found Maksim extremely attractive, adding another complicated element to an already jacked-up situation.

However, before I could give it any more thought, the door to the women's restroom swung open, and my eyes widened as I saw Maksim's reflection in the mirror. I had no idea what he was doing in here, but I whirled around to look at him, positively stupefied.

"What…what are you doing in here?"

Instead of answering me, Maksim grabbed my hand, and I barely had enough time to reach for my purse before he was dragging me out of the women's restroom. I became even more confused when he pulled me into the men's restroom, instead of taking me back to our table, and I couldn't help but blush at the startled faces that looked over at us.

"Get out," Maksim ordered, and I'd never seen men scurry around so quickly.

As soon as the last man cleared the doorway, Maksim was locking the door, and that had me asking, "What are you doing? What is this?"

Maksim crowded me until my back was up against the sink counter, and I wasn't sure if the shiver that ran down my spine was from fear or something else, but whatever was going on right now, it was clear that I was not the one in control. Either Maksim knew that something was wrong, or else he was just showing me how his reputation had been well earned.

"So, what did you come up with, *lyublyu?*" he asked, his voice sounding raspier than before.

"What...what does that mean?" I stammered. *"Lyublyu?"*

"It's Russian for love," he answered, surprising me, though it could easily be something that he called all women. "Now, tell me. What did you come up with?"

"What..." I shook my head a bit in confusion. "What do you mean?"

"Isn't that why you went to the restroom?" he replied, his voice a mocking lullaby. "To come up with an excuse as to leave? To cut our conversation short?"

I could feel my eyes widen.

*How could he have possibly known?*

"N...no," I lied, feeling like a rabbit caught in a trap, which I was when you thought about it.

"Then tell me why you're so nervous, Katja," he ordered as his body heat warmed me from head to toe. "Does my name intimidate you?"

I felt trapped by those empty eyes of his, and it was crazy how a psychopath could be so gorgeous. "Isn't...isn't that what it's supposed to do?"

"Forget my name," he said, ignoring my question. "Tell me what *I* make you feel."

Fear was the correct answer, but I couldn't deny that he was making me feel something else, and if I wasn't here to betray him, then I'd be game to find out what that something else was. However, I *was* here to betray him, and so the rest of it didn't matter.

Nevertheless, my breath caught in my lungs when I felt Maksim's hand slide underneath my dress and between my thighs. His dark eyes held mine as the heat from his palm left a trail on the inside of my right thigh, and my body clenched as he got closer to the apex of my thighs. I knew that I should be stopping him, but this was the whole point of me being here, right? Klive had ordered me to seduce this man, and while I'd come here to do just that, it felt like Maksim was seducing me, not the other way around.

When his fingers finally brushed up against my damp panties, my hands gripped the counter behind me, and I held on tightly as two of his fingers slid inside the gusset of the useless fabric. I should have felt embarrassed by how wet I was, but with the way that Maksim was staring down at me, I didn't feel embarrassed at all. The desire in his eyes had me feeling emboldened, even when I should be fearing for my life.

The second that I felt his fingers slide into my pussy, I closed my eyes, let my head drop back, then let out a low moan. I was letting Maksim Barychev finger fuck me in the men's restroom at The Swan, and while I should be feeling mortified, lust was only allowing pleasure to course through my body right now.

"Oh, God..." I whimpered when I felt his other hand slide up my chest to grip the side of my neck.

"Does that feel good, baby?" he asked, his breath hot on my ear, that damn voice of his making my entire body clench with need. "Do my fingers feel good inside you?"

"Yes..." I choked out, not caring how that made me sound.

Even though Maksim's breathing was a soothing tempo in my ear, I could still hear how slick I was as his fingers were like torturous pistons, going in and out of my body. We could both hear how wet I was, and it was just turning me on more. Like most women, I had a healthy sexual appetite, and it'd been too long. Though common sense was telling me that I was crazy for doing this, my body was begging me to let this man do whatever he wanted to me. It didn't even care that we were in a public place, having taken over the men's restroom.

It wasn't long before I was moaning my shame loud enough for anyone to hear. "I'm...I'm going to cum..." I panted. "Don't stop..."

Maksim's hand tightened around my neck, and my knees weakened with need. "So responsive," he cooed in my ear. "So ready to cum for me, aren't you?"

"Yes..."

"Soak my fingers, baby," he ordered. "Give me something to taste. Give me something to hold me over until I get you into a bed."

I let go of the counter, then grabbed onto his forearm, my nails digging into his flesh as I came all over his fingers, his voice putting me under a spell that I wasn't sure that I could break. In fact, everything about Maksim was everything that I hadn't been expecting, and as my entire soul shook with the orgasm coursing through my body, I knew that I needed to tell him the truth.

*Even if he was going to kill me over it.*

# CHAPTER 9

*Maksim ~*

Katja Volkov was a beautiful woman, but she was absolutely breathtaking when she was cumming for a man. The flush of pleasure that raced up her chest to her cheeks made her look like a wanton piece of art, and I couldn't wait until she was cumming on my cock. Now that she wasn't running from me, I was going to spend the entire night ruining her for all other men.

When I finally pulled my fingers out of her soaked cunt, I brought them up to my lips, and I wasted no time sticking them in my mouth, tasting her for the first time. As predicted, she tasted like I could spend hours with my face in between her thighs, and that's what I planned to do as soon as I got her to a hotel room.

I was just pulling my fingers out of my mouth when Katja finally opened her eyes, and they were glowing like the sun, desire looking incredible on her. Even in a dingy men's restroom with the scent of urine in the air, she looked fucking stunning.

"Are we leaving together, Katja?" I asked, getting straight to the point. "Or would you rather return to our table where we'll pretend that you just didn't cum on my fingers or that my tongue doesn't taste like your pussy?"

Her cheeks turned a bright red, and it looked good on her. "I...I'd like to...to leave together," she stammered a bit. "But...but there's something that I need to tell you."

My back immediately straightened with a simmering anger. If she was married, then we were going to have a problem. It would also explain why she'd been acting nervously at the table earlier. If you could cheat on your spouse without being nervous, then that was the official sign that your marriage was over.

"Are you married?" I asked, anger already lacing the edge of my voice. "Is that what you need to tell me?"

Katja's eyes widened, all that desire giving way to shock. "What? No," she

35

rushed out. "No, I'm not married. What kind of person..." She started shaking her head. "Yeah, no. No, I'm not married."

The pressure in my chest eased a bit, and though she didn't stop me when I reached for her hips, something was still off. "Then what is it, *lyublyu?*"

Suddenly, she seemed to snap out of the moment, her eyes looking troubled again. "Not here," she said.

I arched a brow with confidence, my instincts never wrong. "Did you drive?"

She nodded. "Yes."

Normally, I'd escort a woman, but since I had no idea what this was, I thought it best if she had her car available in case our conversation didn't go well. While she'd said that she wasn't married, there were lots of other things that could become an issue once she confessed whatever it was that she had to say.

"Do you know where The Silk Robe is located?" I asked.

Katja shook her head. "No."

"Do you have a cellphone?"

She blushed. "Of course."

"I'll meet you there," I told her.

Suddenly, she looked unsure, but then quickly grabbed my arm. "Can we...can we walk out of here together? Can you...you walk me to my car? You know, so that it looks like we're together?"

I stared at her, and for some unknown reason, I wanted to put her at ease. I could admit that I'd never felt that particular need with a woman before, and so I wasn't sure what to do with the feeling. At any rate, my curiosity was too strong to ignore, so we were going to see this through, no matter where it led us.

"Of course, *lyublyu.*"

That was another thing that was different. I hadn't ever called a woman by love, calling them doll as a default to calling them by their names. Names hadn't ever been important because I hadn't ever been in it for longer than one night. Granted, it was the same for Katja, but it still felt right calling her love.

Unlocking the restroom door, I held her hand in mine as we made our way through the bar and towards the front door. Even though everyone had their suspicions about what may or may not have happened in the restroom, no one was stupid enough to comment on it. Whatever they thought of Katja, they were going to keep those opinions to themselves.

Once we reached the sidewalk, I escorted her towards the parking lot on the side of the building, and after seeing her safely in her car, I waited until she was on the road before making my way back to my vehicle. As always, I glanced around to make sure that nothing or no one was coming at me from any angle, and when I reached my car, Jurik was already opening the door for me. While I didn't need a guard, I had agreed to one just to satisfy Avgust and

Akim. Agreeing to a guard had been the only way that Akim would also agree to one.

"The Silk Robe," I instructed as I got into the backseat.

On the way to the hotel, I pulled out my phone, then dialed Avgust. Like always, he answered within a couple of rings, probably not wanting to wake the baby or his wife.

"Maksim."

"I am on my way to The Silk Robe," I told him. Though we owned several hotels in the state, The Silk Robe was the one that was guarded the heaviest since lots of the bratva used it.

"Okay," he drawled out. "And I need to know this...why?"

"Though it isn't anything that I cannot handle, the young lady in question was behaving nervously, and before we took things further, she had insisted that we needed to talk," I answered. "With everything that is going on, I thought it'd be best that you know."

"What are you thinking?"

"Nothing definitive yet, but there's something there, and I'm going to find out what it is," I told him.

"Be careful," he warned. "Women can be just as lethal as men."

"Oh, I'm aware," I chuckled.

After hanging up with Avgust, I thought about all the things that this could be, but I knew for certain that this had nothing to do with the Sartoris or O'Briens. Even if we didn't have an unspoken truce right now, neither outfit used women to do their dirty work. Of course, she could be working for someone else, need a favor for her strung-out boyfriend, or just wanted to discuss prices. Honestly, it could be anything, but for her sake, it better not be something that she couldn't walk back from.

When I finally entered the hotel lobby, it was to see Katja sitting patiently on one of the settees that decorated the place, and as I observed her, she seemed more nervous than she'd had when I'd had her locked in the men's restroom earlier. Whatever this was, I was feeling more and more wary about it.

As soon as I approached the settee, Katja was on her feet, fidgeting with her purse strap hung on her shoulder. "Maksim."

Having called ahead after getting off the phone with Avgust, we didn't need to check in at the reception area. Though The Silk Robe was owned by the bratva and was very well protected, I only reserved my rooms through the manager, and I never used the same room twice. For all that we like to preach about loyalty, money would always be a threat to our brotherhood, so a person could never be too careful.

At any rate, if Katja found it strange that we were heading straight for the elevators, she didn't comment on it. Instead, she silently followed me into the steel box, making me wonder what was so important that she'd follow me anywhere without question, even knowing who I was and what I was known for.

Once we reached the top floor, we got out, then headed down the hallway. Still choosing silence, we entered the suite, and when the door shut behind us, I made sure to lock it. With or without Katja here, I always locked any door that I was behind. Now, while most people would assume that the little measure of caution was because of the life that I led, they'd be wrong. I was in the habit of locking my doors because of Naslediye, my cat. She'd gotten out once, and I was man enough to admit that I had searched for the damn thing for hours before I'd finally found her sleeping underneath one of the rose bushes that decorated the left side of my home. I also named her the Russian word for legacy, letting Akim know that she was going to inherit all my wealth if he ever got on my nerves too much.

Forgetting about my damn cat, I made my way over to where Katja was standing in the middle of the room, then asked, "So, what is it that you wanted to tell me?"

With that simple question, her fingers turned white as she gripped the strap of her purse tighter, and I knew that whatever she wanted to say wasn't going to be good.

Letting out a deep breath, she finally asked, "Do...do you know someone...someone named Klive Simpson?"

I had my hand wrapped around her throat, and her body slammed up against the wall before she could bury herself deeper in the grave that I was going to dig for her.

# CHAPTER 10

*Katja ~*

Fear raced to every inch of my body as Maksim's hand threatened to cut off my air, and if I'd thought that I was in over my head before, I could see by the look in Maksim's dark eyes that I'd just signed my own death warrant, and all I could think about was my grandfather when the police told him about how they'd found my body.

"Are you wired?" Maksim snarled in my face.

My eyes widened as I tried to shake my head, but his hold on my neck was strong enough to stop any movement. Still, I managed to choke out the one word that I was hoping could save me. "No."

Not believing me, Maksim let go of my neck long enough to tear my dress off me, and as the material floated to the floor, he snatched my purse from my shoulder. I could only stare at him as he grabbed me by my neck again, then dragged me towards the bathroom, my legs doing their best to cooperate.

Once we were in the bathroom, he tossed my purse on the floor, turned on the shower at full blast, then reached down to yank my heels off my feet. He was big enough that he hadn't needed to let go of my neck, and when he was done with my shoes, he dragged me back into the sitting room, his hold on my neck hard enough to leave bruises.

When he had me back up against the wall, he let go of my neck, but instead of stepping back to give me some room to catch my breath, he flattened his hand against my collarbone, still holding me prisoner. Though this was my fault for agreeing to do this, anger slithered down my spine at the injustice of it all. All I'd wanted to do was save my grandfather, and even if Maksim was satisfied with just killing me, I had no doubt that Klive would go after him.

"You get only one chance at this, Katja," he warned. "So, if I were you, I'd start talking, and I'd make sure to leave nothing out."

39

Doing my best to save my life, I said, "A few days ago, I was having lunch at Trevally's, and this guy just…he just came over and sat down at my table." Maksim's chocolate-colored gaze felt like death coating my skin, and I knew that I needed to make him believe me. "He had an envelope with him, and it was filled with pictures and…and information on me and my grandfather."

"Your grandfather?"

I nodded frantically. "Yes, he…he lives in an assisted-living complex, and…and he's the only family that I have left."

"Let me guess," Maksim drawled out. "He threatened your grandfather's life?"

Tears of anger began to coat my eyelashes. "This isn't a joke," I spat. "Do you honestly think that I'd get involved with the goddamn Russian Bratva if this was a joke? Do you honestly believe that I'd do something like this if I didn't really believe that my life and my grandfather's life were in danger?"

"Finish your story," he ordered, ignoring my minor outrage.

"After…after he sat down, he asked me if I'd gotten the flowers that he'd sent me at work, letting me know that he knew where I worked," I went on. "When I asked him who he was, he said his name was Klive Simpson, but I…I called him out on that because his accent was clearly Russian."

"He speaks with a heavy accent?" Maksim asked, his eyes looking for any lies in my story.

I nodded. "His English is good, but it's clear that English is his second language."

"What else?"

"He said that for the time being, I'd be calling him Klive." I took in a deep breath, trying to calm my racing heartbeat, but I knew that it wasn't going to help. "When I threatened to leave, he asked me what my grandfather would think of my bad manners, and that's when he called me something in Russian."

"Do you remember what he called you?"

I shook my head. "I can't pronounce it," I answered, wondering if it was going to cost me my life. "Anyway, I asked him what he wanted, and that's when he told me that he knew everything about me because he'd done his homework."

"Why did he choose you?"

"I'll…I'll get to that part," I promised. "So, when I asked him again what he wanted, he said that he wanted me to seduce you."

"Seduce me?" he echoed.

I nodded again. "I asked him if he was crazy and told him that you weren't the type to be seduced by feminine wiles, and that he was out of his mind to think that I could pull something like that off."

"And?"

I let out another panicked sigh. "He said that he'd been watching you for a while now, and that he's very familiar with your type."

Maksim's eyes darkened dangerously. "He admitted to watching me?"

"Yes," I answered. "He said that he'd been watching you, and that he knew for a fact that I was your type."

Maksim didn't bother to hide how his eyes slid down my body and then back up again. I was only in my bra and panties, so he could see practically everything. Because my dress had been designed with thin straps, I'd been forced to wear a strapless bra, so my breasts were pushed up and being presented like an offering. Or better yet, a sacrifice.

"He's not wrong," Maksim replied lethally as his eyes were back on mine.

Ignoring that, I said, "When I asked him why me, he claimed that it was just happenstance. Good luck on his part, bad luck on mine. He said that he saw me leaving work one day, and that something about me caught his eye, and that's when he put his plan into action. He said that whatever had captured his attention was bound to capture yours."

"How fortuitous for him that he was right," Maksim remarked, his voice deepening a notch.

Choosing to ignore him again, I went on with my recap of what'd happened. "When I asked him why, he said that his reasons were none of my business. When I refused, he...he said that my grandfather would not live to see next week. When I still refused, he went on to tell me about all the accidents that could befall my grandfather, then gave me a rundown of my grandfather's days at the assisted-living complex."

"Then what?"

"Then he said that if I went to the police or called the living center that...he said that it would take only one phone call, and my grandfather would be dead before I could even file a police report," I continued. "When I...when I asked him what would happen if it didn't work, he said that I better make it work. He said...he said that if I wanted my grandfather to live, then I'd better become the best...uh, that I better be good enough to keep getting invited back to your bed."

"Oh, I'm sure that's exactly how he phrased it," Maksim smirked as he arched a brow condescendingly.

Ignoring the blush on my cheeks, I said, "When I pointed out that you would kill me if you found out, he said that so would he, but unlike you, he'd also kill my grandfather, and that...that I had to decide by today." Maksim hadn't removed his hand, so I kept going, anything to save my life. "When he left, I went back to work, but when I got home that evening, I went through the envelope, and it had everything on me and my grandfather, and even a picture of you."

"What was he hoping to accomplish by this?"

I shook my head. "I don't know," I rushed out. "I think...I think his plan was for me to report back to him or something, but I honestly don't know. In fact, I still hadn't decided what I was going to do, but then I'd gotten a text earlier this evening, telling me that you were at The Swan, and that I better rush over and…and do what he wanted."

Maksim's hand slid slowly back up to wrap around my neck, and his voice sounded like all the demons in hell when he asked, "Is that why you let me finger fuck you in the men's restroom earlier, *lyublyu?* Is that why you came all over my hand? You liked being Klive Simpson's whore?"

My face paled at that, but it was hard to blame him for thinking that. "No," I quickly answered. "No, that had…that was something different."

"Why did you excuse yourself from our table?"

Looking into Maksim's eyes, I knew that he was just waiting for me to lie to him, so that he could kill me with justification, though I seriously doubted that Maksim Barychev felt like he needed to justify his kills. In fact, Maksim Barychev could probably sleep soundly in his bed with the blood of his enemies still on his clothing.

Knowing that it'd be my life if I lied even a little bit, I said, "Because I needed a second to try to come up with a way out of this. It took only five minutes in your company to know that my death at your hands would be a lot worse than whatever Klive Simpson could do to me, so I just…I needed a moment."

"That still doesn't explain why you let me touch you in the restroom, *lyublyu.*"

"Maksim…"

"Or why you'd been so fucking wet," he added, making shame coat my entire face.

# CHAPTER 11

*Maksim ~*

While I was angry, I was most angriest at the fact that Katja was exactly my type, and that Nikel had been correct about that. I did not appreciate that he knew *anything* about me, nor did I appreciate how he'd been closer than we'd all believed.

I also didn't like how Katja had felt so good wrapped around my fingers, and if not for her attack of conscience, then I might not know any of this. I hated how Nikel's trap had worked, and it made me want to snap this beautiful woman's neck in two. It didn't matter that she had changed her mind; she'd gone to The Swan to deceive me, and I wasn't one to give mercy to those that betrayed me.

"When…when I started…started feeling attracted to you, that's when…" Katja let out a troubled sigh. "That's when I excused myself to try to come up with a way out of this."

"Why did you ask me to escort you outside?" I asked, though I already knew the answer. I really just wanted to catch her in a lie because then that would make things so much easier.

"I was scared that Klive might be holed up somewhere, watching," she confessed. "If we'd left separately, he might think that I'd failed and…and I don't know." Tears started welling in those stunning eyes of hers. "He has to have someone watching my grandfather at Windmill Gates, or else how could he know so much? He knows the names of the people that my father talks to and plays chess with." She let out another shuttered breath. "He said that all it'd take is one phone call. Just one."

My first instinct was to just kill her. It would solve all my problems where she was concerned, but since Nikel had no idea that she had betrayed him, her confession could work in the bratva's favor. Instead of Nikel using her to spy on me, we could use her to weed out Nikel Ovchinnikov, once and for all.

As the idea began forming in my head, I could admit that her grandfather may pose as a problem. As long as his life was in danger, then Katja wouldn't be loyal to either Nikel or myself. She was willing to do whatever was needed to keep her grandfather safe, so if I was going to get her to cooperate with us, then I needed to prove that we could keep the only family that she had left alive.

Finally letting go of her neck, I stepped back from her as I pulled out my phone. Not caring that she was in the room, as soon as Bogdan answered, I said, "I need everything that you can find on Katja Volkov. She also has a grandfather named..."

As soon as I shot Katja a look, she said, "Stepan Antonov. He's my mother's father."

"Stepan Antonov," I finished. "I also needed it yesterday."

"Why? What's going on?" he asked warily.

With my eyes on Katja's, I answered, "She's playing the whore for Nikel Ovchinnikov, and I like to know everything that I can about my enemies."

"What?" he practically screeched like a teenage girl. "You've got Ovchinnikov's whore with you?"

"Relax," I instructed. "I'll tell you guys everything later. For now, I just need what you can find on both names."

"Of course," he replied before hanging up.

Though she was in a precarious position, she still had enough fire in her to say, "I don't know who Nikel Ovchinnikov is, but I am *not* his whore."

Sliding my phone back in my pocket, I said, "Nikel Ovchinnikov is Klive Simpson's real name. So, by all accounts, you *are* his whore. After all, you're willing to fuck whoever he tells you to, right?"

Her chin went up at that. "That's not fair."

Angry that I'd felt something for this woman while we'd been in the restroom earlier, I said, "Fair or not, this is what's going to happen, *lyublyu*. You have two choices in this predicament that you've found yourself in-"

"Predicament that I've found myself in?" she hissed. "You say that like I went looking for this. All I did was have lunch while minding my own goddamn business."

"Nevertheless, this is where you are, and you have two choices in the matter, whether you wish it or not," I continued. "You can go back to *Klive*, tell him that you've failed, and then let him kill you and your grandfather, or else you can come work for the bratva, placing you and your grandfather under our protection."

Her face immediately paled, both options unfavorable ones to someone that lived a normal life. Of course, with her grandfather her main priority, she was going to have no choice but to come work for us. However, once she heard the details of her employment with the bratva, I'd see once and for all how committed she was to saving the only family that she had left.

"What...how can you guarantee my grandfather's safety?" she asked, proving that this was going to be a lot easier that I'd thought.

"Easily," I replied smoothly. "Since Klive knows where you live, we can move the both of you into one of the bratva's homes, providing round-the-clock guards and care for your grandfather."

Huge tears immediately began to fall from those sun-kissed eyes of hers. "In exchange for what?"

"Since all that costs money, you'll pay us back with the goldmine between your legs," I answered coldly. "Of course, you'll have to quit whatever job it is that you have now, but I can guarantee that your pussy will make you more money than any regular job ever could." My eyes purposely raked her up and down as I added, "That body of yours is enough to make a man empty out his bank account for you."

Katja looked incensed, even through her tears, but that was probably because I was being disrespectful as fuck. Women were incredible creatures, so it was demeaning to be told that your greatest asset was your pussy. Still, if you were going to use it as a weapon, then give it the credit that it was due, and everything on Katja Volkov could be interpreted as a weapon; a lethal one at that.

"So, either let Klive Simpson kill my grandfather or become a bratva whore?" she spat. "Those are my two choices?"

Walking towards her, I said, "There's also a third option, but I'm not sure if you're up for it."

"I think that is something that I should decide for myself," she replied coolly, trying to be so fucking brave.

"You could become *my* whore," I told her, making her eyes widen again. "Let Klive think that his plan is working, and in return for not killing you where you stand, you give me complete access to that delectable body of yours until I can finally put Klive Simpson six feet under."

Katja's chest started heaving with anxiousness, and like the smart woman that she was, she asked, "And where does option three leave my grandfather?"

"Same as option two," I replied smoothly. "For your cooperation in flushing Nikel Ovchinnikov out, or as you know him, Klive Simpson, the bratva will care for your grandfather both financially and medically."

"You're a bastard," she whispered as she shook her head slightly.

"I'm not the one that let a complete stranger finger fuck me in a men's restroom to get information from them," I countered, making her eyes glitter with shame and hate. "So, pick your poison, *lyublyu*. However, you better make your choice soon as I've other things to attend to right now."

"What's...what's the plan if I choose option three?"

"I'll make a show of spending some time with you outside the bedroom, and you'll report everything that transpires between you and Nikel Ovchinnikov," I answered easily. "However, if you cannot sell the ruse, then you need to be honest with yourself about that, Katja. Whether you want to believe it or not, I *will* kill you if you betray me."

Ignoring that, she asked, "What am I supposed to tell him?"

"If he's been studying me as he said, then he'll know that I would never tell you anything of importance during our first night together," I told her. "So, give him enough sexual details to make him believe that I'm blinded by that sweet cunt of yours, and that should suffice for right now."

Her jaw clenched before asking, "Why not just have someone follow me? Why can't you just...I don't know, catch him following me, and then get him yourself?"

"Because if he is truly watching me, then that's the first thing that he'll be looking for, and I do not want to tip him off," I explained. "When I'm this close to finally finding him, I am not going to let any basic mistakes mess it up."

I watched her run her hands down her face, not caring about her makeup, and it really would be a shame if I had to kill her once it was all said and done. Katja Volkov was too beautiful to kill, and with as tightly as her pussy had held onto my fingers earlier, I knew that she was going to be a phenomenal fuck.

"Which is it going to be, *lyublyu?*"

With the weight of the world swirling around in those amber eyes of hers, she said, "Option three."

I smirked.

I couldn't help it.

"I'll call for you in a few days, and you'd better be ready," I warned her. "I will be spending all night getting my money's worth out of you, so be prepared."

"You're a bastard," she repeated, choking out the whispered curse.

"I know," I replied easily. "I already know."

# CHAPTER 12

*Katja ~*

After I had agreed to Maksim's impossible compromise to save my life and that of my grandfather's, he had ordered me to get dressed, humiliating me further by ordering me around like a regretful mistake. While I'd been putting my dress back on, he'd been going through my phone, sending both my number and the number that Klive had texted me from to his phone.

Once I'd done my best to put my dress back on, I'd had to tie the straps back together because he'd torn them when he had ripped the garment off my body. To add insult to injury, before we'd left the room, Maksim had messed up my hair, then had smeared my makeup to make me look like the whore that I had agreed to play for him. I had walked out of that hotel looking truly used, and I'd never felt so embarrassed in all my life.

As soon as I'd gotten home, I had taken a hot shower, doing my best to scrub the humiliation from my skin, but it'd been no use. I couldn't scrub the decision that I'd made from my life, and even though I would do anything to keep my grandfather safe, I couldn't imagine the horrors that were going to come from being Maksim Barychev's reluctant whore. The nauseating part was that I was actually attracted to the man, and if that wasn't sick, then I didn't know what was.

What had surprised me the most was that I hadn't seen Klive-*or whatever his name was*-all weekend long. I had expected a visit from him on Saturday morning, but when I'd heard nothing, I had decided to go spend the day with my grandfather, and it'd been torture. The happier that he'd seemed, the more that I had died a little inside.

I had also spent all day eyeing everyone that had come close to my grandfather. There'd been so many smiling faces, and any one of them could be working for Klive, and I had almost gone crazy trying to figure out which one of them was in bed with the enemy. At this rate, if I wasn't insane by the end of the week, then it'd be a miracle.

There was also the fact that I wasn't cut out to be a double-crossing spy. Not only hadn't I heard from Klive all weekend long, but I also hadn't heard from Maksim, and I felt like a nervous wreck as I waited to hear from both of them. I was expected to lie to Klive and sleep with Maksim, and I was neither a good liar nor a sex goddess, which was going to end up with me dead in a ditch somewhere eventually.

Before I could think on it some more, my desk phone was ringing, and looking at the extension, it could only be my two o'clock appointment. While most of my job consisted of emergency troubleshooting, it wasn't unheard of to have consultation meetings with clients or potentially new opportunities. There was so much involved with IT that a lot of people liked things explained to them in layman's terms to get a better feel for what we did here.

Picking up the phone, I said, "This is Katja."

"Hey, Katja," Tanisha greeted. "Your two o'clock appointment is here."

"I'll be right down," I told her before hanging up.

Since we all worked in a cubicle setting, there were conference and meeting rooms on the lobby floor, and they were opened to anyone that might need them. All that we had to do was schedule a room with reception, and they kept the appointment book for us.

When I finally walked out of the elevator, my heart stopped in my chest when I saw Klive Simpson waiting for me, and I should have known. When I'd first heard his voice at the restaurant, I should have known. It was the same voice that had scheduled a meeting with me last week, and between the meeting and the flowers, it was clear that Klive had planned this out a while back. He'd already been setting the stage before he had even approached me at lunch, and I felt stupid for not catching on earlier.

As soon as I got close enough, he said, "Ms. Volkov, it is so good to finally meet you."

Having no choice, I took his outstretched hand in mine, then shook it like this was a legitimate business meeting. Even if I'd wanted to cause a scene or send him on his way, I had agreed to act as if everything was normal, and if I messed things up now, Maksim Barychev would be sure to take exception. The plan was for me to act normal, and me losing my shit would not be me acting normal.

"Mr. Simpson," I said, returning his greeting as I let go of his hand. "Would you follow me this way?"

Not waiting for him to answer, I turned to head towards the meeting room that I had reserved last week, and with the walls all floor-to-ceiling glass, I made sure to keep my smile plastered on my face, taking a seat on the other side of the table as professionalism would dictate. The only thing that helped was that the glass was tinted a bit, so my facial expressions might be hidden enough.

Once we were both seated, Klive got right to the point. "What did you learn?"

I couldn't help but look at him like he was stupid, and that wasn't acting on my part. "Are you serious?"

"Why wouldn't I be?" he retorted.

"Do you really think that Maksim Barychev just rolled off me, then started telling me bratva secrets?" I practically spat, resentment for this monster threatening to choke me. "I was lucky enough that he escorted me to my car when he was done with me."

"I told you to impress him," he hissed.

My brows shot upward. "Enough to give me the combination to his safe after a few hours together? Are you delusional?"

Klive's dark eyes flared, and I could tell that he didn't appreciate my logic right now. "Then what did you learn?"

"Nothing," I answered.

"Really?" he mocked. "Because you guys seemed rather cozy at the bar."

*So, he had been watching.*

"He sat down, then introduced himself," I bit out. "I fed him some story about my friend standing me up, then after acting like an idiot that was impressed by his last name, I excused myself to go freshen up." I let out a deep breath, hating that I was going to share the truth with him, but the only way to pull off a successful lie was to stick as close to the truth as possible. "A few minutes after I excused myself, he barged into the women's restroom, then dragged me into the men's restroom where...where we got to know each other a little bit better."

Klive arched a brow. "And how was that accomplished?"

"You don't need the details."

"Oh, but I do," he insisted. "I want to know that you are not lying to me."

I shot him a loathsome look. "He stuck his hand up my dress. Happy?"

"Did he make you cum, *milaya devushka?*"

"What does that mean? What are you calling me?" I asked, instead of answering him.

"It means sweet girl," he answered, surprising me that he'd bother. "Now, tell me. Did he make you cum?"

"Yes," I snapped through clenched teeth. "From there, we went to a hotel, and...and I did everything that I could to make an impression on him."

"Did you let him fuck you up the ass?" he asked, his eyes gleaming with a predatory glint.

"No," I answered. "I wanted to make an impression, so I...I told him that I wasn't ready to trust anyone with that yet. I thought...I thought that if I made him feel like he had to earn it, then he'd call me again."

"Did it work?" he asked, eyeing me carefully, much like Maksim had, trying to spot the lies.

"I don't know," I lied. "He did ask for my number, so I'm thinking that it might have. I mean, why else ask for my number? After all, Maksim Barychev hardly seems the type to bother with a woman's phone number."

Klive leaned back in his seat, mulling over my words. "No, he doesn't," he agreed. "So, if he asked for your number, then I'd say that it worked."

"What is your endgame, Klive?" I finally asked. "I mean, this could take weeks, *months*. Hell, Maksim might never tell me anything at all." I shook my head a bit. "What do you want me to find out *specifically*? Are you looking for his home address? His phone number? What?"

After a few seconds, he finally said, "The plan is to be able to execute Maksim Barychev and his brother, Akim, without it costing me my own life. So, in order for that to happen, I need to find a way in, and you're my way in, Katja."

"What does that even mean?"

"Maksim is going to eventually ask you to meet him somewhere, perhaps even give you the code to his home, office, or give you a hotel key room…*something,*" he explained. "When that happens, that is when I'll strike."

"You're insane," I told him. "Even if you are able to kill Maksim, getting your hands on both Maksim *and* his brother is impossible. Not to mention that you'll be bringing down the wrath of Avgust Kotov down on your head."

*"Milaya devushka,* I welcome it," he replied evenly, proving that he really was crazy.

# CHAPTER 13

*Maksim ~*

After I had sent Katja on her way last Friday, I had immediately called Avgust to tell him what was going on, and I'd ended up going to his place to speak about the situation in person. Luckily for us, Samara and Mitre had already been asleep, and so there'd been no disturbing Avgust's domesticated bliss. Granted, Samara was used to how her husband's world worked, but I still didn't relish disrupting their family time together if I didn't have to.

At any rate, once I'd spoken to Avgust about everything, he had insisted on another meeting with Akim in attendance as well as Bogdan's completed background check on Katja and her grandfather. Avgust had also suggested reaching out to Nero Sartori for Morocco's Carrisi's hacking skills, but since Katja had been a free fountain of information, I was still confident that a simple background check would suffice for what we were looking for. If things became more complicated later on, then we could look into using Morocco has a resource again.

So, with Bogdan's background check completed, and Akim now in on what was going on, we were all at my place, ready to discuss what to do next.

"This motherfucker has some nerve," Akim remarked, still trying to process what we'd just told him only moments ago. "I mean, seriously."

"I do not understand why your cat hates me," Avgust murmured pensively, eyeing Naslediye.

"She does not hate you," I told him for the millionth time. "She just doesn't like people invading her space."

"This is *your* house," Avgust retorted. "She should know that she is not in charge."

"Don't take it personally," Akim chimed in. "She hates us all."

"Can we get back to Nikel Ovchinnikov?" I drawled out, getting off the subject of my cat and her antisocial ways.

"Well, Bogdan's background checks on her and the grandfather came back

51

simple and boring," Avgust announced, something that we both already knew and were just making Akim aware. "There is nothing sinister in her past, though the tragedy of losing her parents and grandmother is unfortunate."

"Nonetheless, I do not like the idea of having to trust a perfect stranger," I replied.

"True," Akim agreed. "However, you have to give her points for coming clean, Maksim. I know that you don't want to, but she could have said nothing."

"We're simply the lesser of two evils," I pointed out.

"The evil that can guarantee her grandfather's safety." Avgust said. "In fact, it's her grandfather that we need to concentrate on, not her."

"How do you mean?" Akim asked.

"He means that with her grandfather in poor health, we can manipulate her loyalty by taking care of him more than threatening him," I explained, mine and Avgust's brains usually on the same wavelength. "If she sees him being protected and taken care of, that will mean more to her than any fear that she may feel over endangering his life. Remember, women are emotional creatures, and if you can make them feel something good, there's almost nothing that they won't do for you. Why do you think diamonds and flowers work so effectively after a man has beaten or cheated on his wife? It's because they'd rather live in the moment of euphoria than live in the hard truth of hurt."

"Well, that's stupid," Akim retorted.

"Stupid or not, it's the truth," I went on. "We give Katja nothing by threatening her grandfather the same way that Nikel did. However, if she sees how we are adding value to her grandfather's life and hers, then she'll never betray us for Nikel."

"And you really believe her about their meeting being a mere coincidence?" Akim asked, and I didn't blame him. After all, the story was pretty farfetched.

"Though Nikel could have been lying about that, I believe that Katja thinks it to be the truth," I answered. "I'm more concerned with knowing that he's been close enough to observe us without us knowing."

"Which could only mean that he's wearing a rather convincing disguise," Avgust remarked evenly, though I knew that he had to be just as irritated as I was. "All our men know his picture, and everyone is actively looking for him."

"Yet we still don't know where he is staying, or where he's getting his money," Akim added. "We even checked the borders, and he was still nowhere to be found."

"He has to be staying with a woman," I said. "Women are caregivers by nature, so if someone is supporting him, it has to be a woman. A woman that works but appreciates whatever he does for her at home that she isn't insisting that he provide financial help." I started flicking my fingers, an old habit that didn't make an appearance often. "It's also possible that he has more money than we're giving him credit for. After all, we really don't know how long he and his cohorts had been in Port Townsend before that first guy met his demise with the Sartoris."

"Well, if he's watching us, then we just have to look for someone that doesn't belong," Akim suggested.

"If we start acting like we know that he's watching us, then that'll tip him off," I pointed out. "Just like Nikel is hoping that Katja can catch me slipping, we're hoping for the same thing. If Nikel trusts her, he might just let his guard down long enough for us to catch him."

"Did you show her the picture of Nikel to confirm that it's the same person?" Akim asked, looking between me and Avgust. "I mean, how do we even know it's the same guy. While Morocco is good at what he does, who's to say that Nikel hasn't had some plastic surgery work done or something.'

Avgust's eyes slid my way. "He has a point."

"Well, seeing as how I was doing my best not to snap Katja's neck when she confessed to working for Nikel, it slipped my mind," I drawled out. "However, I'll be sure to show her his picture the next time that I see her."

"Which is?" Avgust asked.

"Ideally, I'd like to meet up with her tomorrow or Wednesday, but that might tip my hand," I answered. "I need to be interested in her just enough, but nothing too obvious."

"I really do not like this," Avgust remarked. "I do not like that he has eyes on you, but we do not know what he looks like."

"Once I show Katja the picture, I'm sure it'll be easier to find him," I assured him.

Eyeing both me and Akim, Avgust said, "Until then, I want both of you to travel with no less than two guards."

"No way," Akim immediately objected.

"That wasn't a suggestion, Akim," Avgust informed him, and there was really only one thing that Akim could say to that.

"Of course, Pakhan."

"It's only for a week," Avgust said, trying to soothe Akim's ruffled masculinity.

Ignoring them both, I said, "Katja said that he approached her at Trevally's. Maybe we can have Morocco do his thing with the city cameras again."

"Yeah, why can't we do that?" Akim chimed in, in complete agreement with the idea.

"I'm not sure that Nero would be willing to lend Morocco out to us again," Avgust answered. "He was absolutely clear about the reasons for his generosity last time, so unless Maksim is in love with Katja, I can't see him being so understanding this time around. Remember, we are not friends."

My brother looked at me. "Are you in love with her?"

I shot him a look. "I barely know the woman," I reminded him. "Plus, did you miss the part where she's in bed with Nikel Ovchinnikov?"

Akim ran his hands down his face. "What a fucking mess."

"You're not wrong," I muttered.

"Wait," Akim announced. "Won't we be tipping our hand if he notices that her grandfather suddenly has guards or new nurses?"

"I thought about that," I told him. "We're going to move her grandfather back in with her, and while his nurses will be actual nurses, they'll also have a live-in 'housekeeper' that will actually act as her grandfather's guard. If Nikel questions how she can afford all the new changes, she can tell him the truth."

"Which is?" Akim asked.

"That I'm paying her for pussy," I answered. "If I'm supposed to be so enthralled with her talents in the bedroom, then it would stand to reason that I might provide for her financially."

"If you can find a way to 'bump' into her before the weekend, do it," Avgust ordered. "I do not like waiting now that we're so close to finally catching him."

"Of course, Pakhan," I automatically replied.

"I need a goddamn drink," Akim grumbled, and he wasn't the only one.

In fact, I probably needed a few.

# CHAPTER 14

*Katja ~*

I was becoming a complete basket case, and I didn't know how to get out of my head long enough to calm the hell down. I still hadn't heard from Maksim, and so my conversation with Klive felt like a ticking bomb inside my brain, my mind worried that I might forget something.

At any rate, with panic eating at my insides, I decided to go visit my grandfather to remind myself of why this was all worth it. Even though he was never far from my mind, I needed an extra dose of strength to see this disaster through. In all my life, I hadn't ever imagined that I'd get embroiled in a criminal espionage, so I hadn't trained for this shit, hysteria something that I found myself battling daily since the day that Klive Simpson approached me.

Practically on autopilot, I pulled into the parking lot of Windmill Gates, got out of my car, hit the key fob to lock it, then made my way through the lobby to find my grandfather. While I was early and would probably catch him during dinner, I didn't care. I needed to see him, and I also knew that he wouldn't mind the interruption. Besides, it wouldn't be the first time that I'd eaten in the eatery with him and his new friends.

However, before I could go looking for him, Devers Branch was making her way towards me, stopping me. "Katja, I'm so glad I caught you."

"Hello, Mrs. Branch," I greeted. "How are you?"

"Oh, I'm fine, child," she answered kindly. "I'm always fine."

I smiled at that. "Well, what can I help you with?"

"I just wanted to tell you that we are going to miss your grandfather terribly," she said, surprising me. "Mr. Antonov is such a delight, and he's made our lives better by knowing him."

Doing my best to act like I knew what she was talking about, I said, "Yeah, he...he really loves this place."

Her face quickly softened. "Well, you know...when we first heard that you

55

were taking Mr. Antonov home with you, some of us were immediately worried that something had happened, or that you might feel as if he wasn't getting the proper care here," she said. "But when Mr. Dubie assured us that you were simply taking him home because you were able to afford his personal care now…well, while we were all happy for the both of you, we're still going to miss him so much."

"He's definitely going to miss everyone here," I assured her, my mind spinning at how Maksim had already arranged for my grandfather to come home, yet hadn't even called me to tell me. "Plus, if he ends up deciding that he prefers the comfort of his new community to sitting home with just me to entertain him, we can always see about bringing him back here."

*I was rambling.*

Suddenly, I realized that I had no idea what I was doing. Once the Kotovs captured Klive Simpson, my grandfather and I were no longer going to be in danger, and then what? I couldn't see Maksim Barychev paying for my grandfather's care indefinitely, and since I wouldn't be able to afford it on the salary that I made now, would I have to whore myself out to Maksim until my grandfather finally found peace in the afterlife? Then there was also no guarantee that Windmill Gates would have any rooms available whenever the money dried up. I'd made demands without thinking them through, and it wasn't lost on me how it'd be in my best interest for the Kotovs *not* to find Klive Simpson.

I could feel a bubble of hysteria making an appearance, so I quickly said, "Well, I need to go find my grandfather, Mrs. Branch. We'll be sure to say our goodbyes to everyone when we finally get around to moving him home."

She graced me with a genuine smile that made me feel like crap. "Of course, Katja."

Turning from her, I went in search of my grandfather, and when I found him reading quietly underneath the big oak near his bungalow, my heart thumped painfully in my chest. He looked so damn peaceful, and a part of me wondered if I was making a mistake by taking him away from all of this. Of course, with his safety the priority, I was confident about *why* I was taking him home with me, but was he going to miss the social interaction that this place provided for him? Was he going to be lonely while I worked all day? Plus, now that I had to pay for his safety by spreading my legs for Maksim, was that going to make my grandfather lonely during the evenings as well?

Tears were quickly making an appearance as the weight of confusion threatened to crush me. I no longer knew what the plan was, and it was killing me to think that I didn't even have enough sense to do something as simple as taking care of my grandfather.

When I finally approached his chair, I said, "Hey, *Dedushka.*"

He placed his book on his lap, his light brown eyes regarding me carefully. "I hear that I am going home," he said, cutting to the chase. "How is that possible, *dorogoy*? How is that you can afford such a thing?"

I took a seat on the bench next to his chair, and hating myself inside, I was going to do my best to convince him of my lies, praying that it worked. After all, this was the man that knew me best, and I'd never been able to lie to him before without getting caught. My grandfather might be eighty-three, but he was still as sharp as a tack, and that was going to make this so much more difficult.

"Well, first off, it was supposed to be a surprise," I lied. "I wanted to be the one to tell you, but I forgot to let Mr. Dubie know that, and for that I'm sorry. You should have heard the news from me."

"I am more interested in how you can afford this, Katja," he repeated. "We did the math until we couldn't see straight, and so I know how much the care costs."

"The Tremaine Group got a new CEO about three months ago, and…well, he seems like a real for-the-people kind of boss," I said, the lies feeling like broken glass on my tongue. "He's the great-grandson of Kenneth Tremaine, and according to the gossip at work, he claims that he has more millions than he and his family will ever need, so he wants to give back to the employees."

Now, everything that I was telling my grandfather about The Tremaine Group was true, except for the part where the new CEO was handing money out like Chicklets. While our new boss was still fairly new, it'd be a couple of years before we could see what kind of boss he'd really be. Passing down the reins was never an easy thing to do, and it really was anyone's guess on what we'd be getting when it was all said and done.

"Really?" he asked skeptically, and since this was America, I didn't blame him.

I nodded. "His father finally stepped down, and once Darren Tremaine took over, he opened the checkbook, and then just started giving away money. Everyone in the company got a twenty-percent raise *and* we get quarterly bonuses now." Guilty tears sprung to my eyes, but I forced myself to smile through them. "You can finally come home."

"Katja, I'd love nothing more than to be home with you," he said, his voice firm but soft. "I miss seeing your grandmother everywhere. Still, I do not want to be a burden-"

"You could never be a burden," I rushed out as I grabbed his hands. "You can't possibly know how much I miss having you at home, and as soon as we got those raises and bonuses, I did the math to see if we could get you home, *Dedushka.*"

"If I were a stronger man, I'd tell you to use all that extra money to do something nice for yourself," he sighed tiredly. "However, I miss your *babushka* so much. I'd like to be home where I can be closer to her."

"And what of the friends that you've made here?" I asked, letting go of his hands, so that I could wipe my eyes.

"I will miss them," he admitted. "I've been treated well here, but if given the choice, I'd rather be home than anywhere else in the world, Katja."

"Well, I'm going to have you home as soon as possible, but since it'll take a few more days to get the nurse's schedule organized, you'll have some more time to spend with your friends," I said, knowing that I was going to have to call Maksim to ask him what in the hell was going on.

My grandfather eyed me, his gaze a knowing one. "Are you sure that everything is okay with you, Katja? You seem…weighted down."

Though I couldn't tell him the entire truth, I was honest when I said, "Now that you're able to come home, I realize just how much I've missed you, *Dedushka*. I feel…I feel both relieved and saddened by how long you've been here."

"Katja, do not do that to yourself," he replied graciously. "I've been treated well here. Truly."

I quickly wiped the quiet tears that I just couldn't seem to get rid of, then said, "Enough of this. I say that we tour the place, get phone numbers, addresses…whatever for the people that you'd still like to keep in touch with."

My grandfather smiled over at me. "I think that's a great idea. I'd really like to see Mrs. Turnbuckle's great-granddaughter grow up. Plus, there's online chess. Gary Reasons cannot cheat if it's online."

Despite the shitshow that was my life, I chuckled. I'd wanted to be reminded of why I was doing all this, and my grandfather's laughter had done just that.

# CHAPTER 15

*Maksim ~*

When Katja had called me the other day to ask about her grandfather, I hadn't answered. Knowing her schedule the way that I did, I had simply texted her when the nurse would start, and what day and time that she would need to be at Windmill Gates to help collect Mr. Antonov. The plan was for him to be moved this Sunday, giving her plenty of time to clear out the third bedroom in their house for their live-in nurse that would also act as a guard to Mr. Antonov, deciding against employing too many people.

Now, though she hadn't texted back, she hadn't needed to. I'd given Katja everything that she needed to know, so a conversation hadn't been necessary. However, when I had texted her this morning to be ready at eight tonight, she had texted back, asking me what to wear. I'd texted that she could wear whatever she wanted, considering that she wouldn't be wearing it for long. I'd made my expectations of tonight clear, so her showing up had been all the consent that I needed.

I stood outside the club, watching the black sedan with Katja in the back pulling up to the curve. Millie's was a bratva gentlemen's club, and not the kind with stripper poles. Million-dollar deals were made here, and everything in the place screamed wealth and class. The place was basically one large boardroom with discreet entertainment. There was a full-service bar, accessible cocktail waitresses, and a couple of rooms in the back that were available to rent.

However, the real gem of the place was the showcase room. It was located on the second floor, and it was essentially a hotel suite. When you walked in, there was a sitting room to the right, and it was decorated with a cream-colored couch, a couple of end tables, a small coffee table, and it faced the huge bed that was to the left of the room. The sitting room also came with a free-standing bar and small refrigerator that came equipped to help you make whatever drink of your choosing.

As for the bed, it was a California King and took up most of the left side of the room. There were two nightstands on either side of the expensive bed, and off to the left was a door that led to a small bathroom. The room was to freshen up only, no large tub or anything like that. It had a small sink area, a toilet, and a shower that was barely wide enough to fit two people. All in all, it was functional enough, and it was also decorated with the same tasteful scheme as the rest of the club, though with one major difference.

*The walls.*

Except for the wall that the headboard rested against, they were all two-way mirrors, and it was the room that Melor used to introduce new bratva whores. Now, while we had plenty of kryshas that volunteered for the job, before he'd gotten married, Melor had been known to indulge every now and again if the girl had been of any interest to him. However, for the most part, our kryshas did the honors.

Anyhow, on the opposite sides of the mirrors were observation rooms. They were small, and we had eight in total that formed an arch around the suite. Whenever we had someone new to present, we turned on the activation light, signaling to the patrons of the place that a showing was going to take place. Though it wasn't quite an auction where we took bids, it did showcase the young lady's talents, and that determined her price range. Surprisingly, a lot of women wanted to go straight for the gold, so they didn't hold back when in the room. More often than not, there were usually a few men in the room with the new prospect, and it couldn't be said that our whores didn't make good money.

At any rate, Katja was the next whore on stage. Her grandfather's care wasn't cheap, and this would give her a choice once it was all said and done. Though I had no doubt that Nikel would be taken care of soon enough, if she wanted to keep her grandfather with her at home indefinitely, then she was going to have to earn the money for that somewhere, and men's need for pussy would never go out of style. There was also the fact that this would be a first for me, catapulting Katja into the most coveted whore on our menu.

As soon as the car stopped at the curve, I walked over, then opened the door for her. If Nikel had eyes on us, then he was going to see me treating Katja like she mattered, and while she might have when I'd first met her, her association with Nikel had ended all that. Trust was the most important thing in the bratva, and she'd admitted to agreeing to betray me before her common sense had gotten the better of her. That moment of culpability was enough to not ever trust her.

Without a word, Katja took my hand, and when she exited the vehicle, her beauty was something that would never be in question. Her black hair was pinned up with loose strands accenting her perfect face, and her makeup was subtle and applied flawlessly. Those golden doll eyes of hers were bright and captivating, and enough to drive a man to his knees.

However, as I looked my fill, she'd chosen a dress that'd been designed to turn heads and make men stupid. It was white that shimmered with each step, and the fabric hugged every curve of her body. While the neckline was modest and the sleeves reached her wrists, the hem stopped mid-thigh, and the matching white shoes made her look angelic. I wouldn't have been surprised if the dress had come with a pair of wings, instead of a matching purse.

Instead of telling her that she was beautiful, I grabbed her hand, then linked her fingers in mine, making a show of it. Again, if Nikel had eyes on us, then I wanted him to believe that his plan was working. I wanted him to believe that I was none the wiser, and that Katja was still in his pocket.

As we headed into the club, I ignored everyone that was trying to get my attention, then continued to lead Katja to the second floor. She didn't say anything, and I wondered if it was because she was nervous or if it was because she really had nothing to say. After all, we weren't dating, so banal chitchat did seem ridiculous.

Once we got to the second landing, I hit the switch to the left of the hallway-*signaling that a show was about to begin*-then escorted Katja down the long corridor to the door at the end. Using the keypad, I opened the door, then placed my hand on the small of her back to move her along. Again, she wasn't saying anything, but what was there to say?

When I turned the inside light on, I heard Katja's small gasp, and it could have been from the beauty of the room or because of the huge bed, but I wasn't curious enough to ask.

"Would you like something to drink?"

She was standing in the middle of the sitting area, and when she turned around to look at me, I was immediately hit with how wrong she looked inside this room. For all of its expensive décor, it was no match for her stunning beauty, and Katja Volkov would put any wonderous landscape to shame with how lovely she truly was.

"Do you have any tequila?"

My brows rose in surprise. "What happened to the wine?"

Her gaze was sure as she said, "I have a feeling that tonight calls for something stronger."

Not bothering to agree or disagree, I headed over to the bar, then poured her a shot of tequila. She didn't say anything as she walked over to grab her liquid courage, and I left her to it as I removed my jacket and guns. No one needed to see where I kept them on my person, and our audience would see just that if I waited until the show began to undress.

After placing my guns in one of the nightstands near the bed, I turned to face Katja again, and she looked like she wanted another drink. I understood her being nervous, but she'd made her choice, and so I expected her to honor her word.

Wanting to make sure that my expectations were clear before I hit the switch for the shades on the other side of the mirrors, I said, "While you may believe that you are here for me to fuck, that is not true."

Her head reared back in surprise. "What?" Her bright eyes started darting around a bit. "I'm not here for…for you?"

"I do not share, Katja," I quickly corrected her. "As long as you're spreading your legs for me, there will be no one else. I do not get turned on by watching or allowing other men to fuck who I am entertaining at the moment."

I watched her throat work nervously. "Then…then what am I doing here if…if not-"

I put my hand up to stop her. "You are here to audition for me," I clarified. "Your grandfather's care is not cheap, and so you are here to prove to me that you're worth the cost and trouble." Her back snapped straight, and that fire in her really did enhance her beauty. "You're here to prove to me that you have what it takes to be just the kind of whore that I would spend thousands on. You're here to prove that you can please me in all the ways that I want to be pleased." I cocked my head a bit, enjoying the quiet anger that danced in her eyes. "You're here to show me all the reasons why I should keep you around, instead of just putting a bullet in your gorgeous head for daring to agree to Nikel's arrangement."

"And…and if I can't?" she asked between clenched teeth. "What…what happens if you're…you're disappointed?"

"Have you forgotten that I already know what your pussy tastes like?" I taunted, reminding her of our encounter in the restroom. "If you fail tonight, then it's because you didn't try, *lyublyu.*"

Instead of replying to that, she asked, "How many chances do I get?"

"Only one, baby," I answered truthfully. "Only one."

# CHAPTER 16

*Katja ~*

I'd never felt so devalued as I did in this moment. I was actually going to whore myself out to Maksim Barychev, and if that wasn't enough to make me feel like my life was no longer mine, if I wasn't good at it, then I'd be discarded like trash, my grandfather and I back where we started from.

I wanted to cry.

I wanted to scream.

"Are you ready?" he asked, that hoarse voice of his sounding like a dangerous dare.

Knowing that I really didn't have a choice, I nodded. While my grandfather could continue to live at Windmill Gates, this was about his safety, and I'd do anything to make sure that nothing happened to him. I just had to keep remembering what was at stake here. If Klive, Nikel, or whatever his name was didn't kill him, Maksim had no reason not to, if just to torment me for how I had agreed to help Klive when he had first approached me. Plus, it wasn't like I was a virgin or believed that sex should only be with someone that you loved. That dream was for young girls that still believed in fairytales.

Taking in a deep breath, I walked over to where Maksim was standing by the bed, and I watched him hit a switch, though I wasn't sure what it did since no lights turned off or on. Stil, a random switch was the least of my problems right now. I needed to prove to Maksim that I was worth the effort in bed, and I wasn't even sure how to do that. While I'd had my fair share of relationships, they'd been normal ones, so I'd had normal sex. Though satisfying, I'd never had porn-star sex. No cumming on my face, no choking me, no calling me names, or anything like that. I'd also never had anal sex before, and I knew that Maksim was going to be expecting it. After all, was a whore even a whore if she didn't give up the ass?

When I was finally standing in front of him, my mouth went dry with how nervous I was. I was going to have to guess what he liked because I knew that I wasn't going to get any help from him. If this was an audition, then I was going to have to make him want me, not the other way around.

With my eyes locked on his dark gaze, I reached back, unzipped my dress, then slowly peeled the soft material from my body, letting it fall to the floor in a graceful dance. Like a clumsy amateur, I left my heels on because I knew that could be a thing for men, and maybe Maksim was one of those men.

"*Lisus Khristos,*" Maksim muttered as his eyes raked down my body.

I'd worn a black lace bra and panty set, the best lingerie that I'd had in my drawer. Being practical, I usually wore functional underclothes because I had a lot to hold up and keep in. However, when Maksim had made his intentions clear earlier, I'd had a feeling that he wouldn't have appreciated basic cotton underwear.

Knowing that I couldn't put this off any longer, my shaky hands reached for his belt, and the tension in the room felt suffocating. For the first time in my life, I wasn't going to have sex for the pure pleasure of it. For the first time in my life, I was going to be playing the whore for a man that had absolutely no respect for me, and could I blame him? After all, Maksim didn't know me. He had no idea what was at the heart of me, and so all that he saw was someone that had agreed to betray him, never mind that I had changed my mind.

After I unbuckled his belt and unbuttoned his slacks, I sank to my knees as I grabbed the waistband of both his pants and underwear, pulling them down far enough for his dick to spring free, the appendage so hard and big that it bounced against his abs. Whatever I'd been expecting, it hadn't been that Maksim would be so beautifully built like this. I also knew that I was going to fail spectacularly at this, and that brought unwanted tears of despair to my eyes. Even if I hadn't gone so long without sex, there was no way that his dick wasn't going to do some serious damage, and so there was no way that I was going to be able to go all night like a seasoned working girl. Plus, I had no doubt that Maksim's sexual past was littered with women that had serviced that thing well.

I finally reached for the base of his dick, and when I looked up at him, a single tear quickly escaped, so I jerked my head back down, hoping that he hadn't seen it, though I was positive that he'd had. However, determined to see this through, I leaned forward, opened my mouth, then swallowed him as far back as I could.

"Fuck," he hissed as I felt one of his hands gripped the back of my head.

I almost laughed.

I wasn't sure what he was doing, but we both knew that this was going to be the least exciting blowjob of his life. There was no way that I was going to be able to take all of him, something that I was certain someone had been able to do for him in the past.

Doing my best to forget everything else, I closed my eyes, then used my tongue to massage the sensitive ridges underneath his cock. While I didn't have much room because he was so thick, I did my best with what I had to work with, and when it was clear that I needed more help, I pulled my lips off his length, then spat on it to get some friction going.

"Fuck, baby," he moaned, his fingers fisting in my hair, messing up how I'd painstakingly pinned it up. "Show me how much you love sucking my cock."

With my hand working the base, I went back to wrapping my lips around his heat, and ignoring how my jaw was going to be sore in the morning, I sucked his dick like I wanted to be down here. I used my hand, lips, and tongue to work him over, and I did my best to pretend that this meant something. If I had any chance of impressing him, then I had to act as if the pleasure was mutual. Prostitutes not only got paid for sex, but they also got paid to manipulate a man's ego like a pro. They were paid for a created fantasy that catered to making a man feel like a king, and that's what I needed to do. I needed to make Maksim feel like he was the only one; I knew this.

I wasn't sure how long I sucked him deep before I felt his fingers tighten painfully in my hair, and before I knew it, Maksim was jerking his hips back, setting me free. When I looked up at him, he looked like a man possessed, and I barely had time to register what was happening when I felt the first rope of hot cum hit my neck. I couldn't do anything but stare up at him as he painted my neck and chest with his seed, the warm thickness searing me like nothing that I'd ever experienced before.

When he was finally done, he said, "Stand up."

On shaky legs, I did as he'd ordered, and once I was standing before him, Maksim took his right hand, then started smearing his cum all over me. My chest was heaving, and I could barely breathe as his dark gaze bore into mine, the wet sounds of his seed smothered all over my skin hitting my ears like a bomb exploding.

Once he was finished marking me, he instructed, "Take off the heels."

Though that surprised me, I quickly kicked them off, wondering if I'd already made a grave error with this man. Granted, I'd already surmised that I wasn't going to pass his test, but I never imagined that a pair of shoes would be my undoing.

Without bothering to zip himself up, Maksim walked behind me, and I felt like I was going to have a heart attack when I felt his hands on the strap of my bra. Doing my best not to hyperventilate, I stood still as he unsnapped the lace, then helped push the material over my shoulders, then down my arms. Since my breasts were fairly large, I felt their weight drop without the support, and with the walls being reflective glass, I was able to see the teardrop shapes on full display.

Still refusing to move an inch, my breath hitched as I felt Maksim reach for my panties, then pull them over my hips, then down my legs, and that's when it dawned on me why he had ordered me to get rid of the shoes.

Looking at my reflection, I was fully naked now, my breasts bare, and my smooth pussy lips visible underneath the small triangle of hair that I always kept trimmed.

*I was fully naked, and he was not.*

I closed my eyes when I felt Maksim's warm breath against my ear. "I want you to climb on the bed, spread your legs, then show me how you pleasure yourself."

I could feel the blush of humiliation race across my skin. While I wasn't a stranger to solo-loving, that was something that was extremely private to me. It was something that I could do without any judgement from anyone; it was a time and place where none of my fantasies were wrong. It was when I was at my most vulnerable because I could be the real me, feeling what I really wanted to feel, and Maksim was going to take that away from me.

"You're going to get on that bed, spread your pussy lips open, so that I can see how pretty it all is, then you're going to play with it to show me what you like," he went on, making me question why he was doing this.

"Why would you care what I like?" I asked without thinking.

"I don't care, baby," he replied brutally. "I just want to see your cunt cum."

With that harsh reminder of why I was here, I climbed onto the bed, then did as he'd instructed. I got comfortable in the middle of the bedding, the pillows positioned perfectly to prop me up. Then, with every ounce of courage that I possessed, I planted both my feet on the bed, then let my knees fall open, showing him everything.

"What are you waiting for?" he asked darkly, a quiet warming in his voice.

I closed my eyes, then did something that no one else had ever seen me do before.

# CHAPTER 17

*Maksim ~*

When I'd said that Katja was beautiful enough to drive a man to his knees, I hadn't been lying. However, when she had looked up at me from her knees, her eyes swimming in tears, that'd nearly been my undoing. I'd seen her eyes filled with tears of anger, fright, and embarrassment, but never tears of hopelessness, and I'd never seen anything so fucking beautiful. Strong women were an aphrodisiac that most men couldn't resist. However, a strong woman that broke as gracefully as Katja was something rare.

I had also underestimated how stunning that fucking body of hers was. At the hotel, I'd been too enraged to really appreciate her incredible figure, but I wasn't enraged now. When her dress had pooled around her feet, it'd been all that I could do not to fall to my knees and just worship her. Of course, the stars that were tattooed on my body forbade such a thing, but in the privacy of our own home, I wouldn't have cared about any of that.

At any rate, as I began to undress, I couldn't take my eyes off the way that Katja was playing with her pussy, the fingers on one hand dancing through her slick folds, her other hand cupping one of her full breasts, and before this night was over, I was going to fuck those magnificent tits of hers.

Transfixed, I had no conscious thought of removing my clothes as Katja played with her pussy, her body arching beautifully every time that her clit sang. Her legs wouldn't stay still, and though her moans were low, I could still hear them. While she might not want to be here, and while she might not want to be doing this, her biological pleasure was undeniable. Every touch felt good, and she probably hated herself for that.

"Make yourself cum," I ordered, my voice deeper than usual. "I want to see that sweet pussy of yours dripping on the bed."

With my cock hard against my abs again, I watched as Katja made herself cum, and if I'd thought that she was beautiful before, that was nothing compared to what she looked like now. This wasn't like when we'd been in the restroom at The Swan. There, we'd both been fully clothed, and what we'd done had been lewd by all accounts. She'd been a woman being finger fucked in the men's restroom, so this was definitely something different. Though still lewd, she was still a piece of art.

"Oh, God…" she choked out when she finally came, and I wanted nothing more than to lick her pussy clean. However, I hadn't forgotten who I was.

As she came down from her high, I walked over to the nightstand, grabbed one of the condoms in the drawer, then put it on in record time, detesting the need for it for the first time in my life. I wanted to *own* Katja Volkov, and a condom prevented that. Nonetheless, that didn't mean that I couldn't defile her everywhere else.

Ideally, I'd be getting on the bed with my back to the wall, so that everyone could see me fucking her, but that wasn't going to work for me. I'd be on my knees, and I couldn't have that. So, instead of jumping her like I wanted to, I said, "Come here, then get on your hands and knees, baby."

Katja turned her head to look at me, her sun-kissed eyes glowing with desire, and if I didn't know better, I'd say that she was high, but she wasn't. It was nothing more than a good orgasm making her forget all the bad things in her life right now. The pleasure derived from an orgasm was a gift from God, and done right, it could make you forget damn near anything.

I crooked my finger at her, and that's when she finally remembered why she was here. However, to my surprise, Katja crawled over to me, and my dick had never been harder. With her round ass perched high, her huge tits swinging beautifully, and her gold-colored eyes peering up at me from underneath her lashes, she crawled to me like a fucking goddess, and I could feel a rush of anger dance down my spine at the thought of her crawling to another man like this. She looked like a rare jungle cat, and I couldn't stop the growl from my throat at how I'd been stupid enough to allow others to see her like this. I'd made a mistake, and I was man enough to be able to admit it.

Nevertheless, I couldn't stop now. Even if I didn't want her more than I wanted to take my next breath, we were men of our word, and I had flipped the switch on this show. To cut it short now would suggest uncertainty on my part, something that I'd never admit to anyone outside the top hierarchy of the bratva.

When she was finally in front of me, I grabbed the back of her head by her hair, then positioned my cock against her lips. Even though she had just made herself cum, Katja wasn't here because she wanted me, and I understood that. So, because I was so thick, it was possible that I might tear her apart once I got inside her since she wasn't genuinely turned on.

"Spit on it," I ordered. "Get it nice and wet, baby."

She did as I'd told her, and satisfied with her work, I gave her a tight nod. With no need to vocally instruct her, Katja turned around on her hands and knees, and like a real whore, she positioned herself face down and ass up, and she really did have the prettiest cunt that I'd ever seen.

After dropping a bead of spit on her asshole, I watched it drip down to her pussy, and when her tight hole clenched, that's when I couldn't take it anymore. I grabbed her hips, then slammed home in one thrust, the feeling of her wrapped around my dick making me see stars.

"Oh, God…" she choked out as her hands fisted the blanket.

Ignoring her cries of discomfort, I let my cock ruin her cunt for all other men. I rammed into her hard and deep, my thick cock splitting her wide open, her pussy lips like a vise around every inch that I was plowing into her. I wanted to rip off the condom, but even as out of my mind as I felt, I still knew better. If I did that, then I'd be done for, and that wasn't going to happen here. When I finally flooded her womb, it was going to be in my bed with just the two of us.

"Take that cock," I grunted behind her, my fingers digging into her hips. "Show me how good you take every fucking inch, baby."

"Maksim…oh, God…" she panted. "Oh, God…"

Letting go of one of her hips, I reached out, grabbed a fistful of her hair, then yanked her upwards. "Tell me what a good little whore you are," I ordered in her ear. "Tell me what a good girl you can be for me, baby."

I felt her hands reach back and latch onto my hips, trying to hold onto anything. "Maksim…"

"Do you feel that?" I taunted. "Do you feel how deep my cock is sliding inside you?"

"Yes…" she whimpered. "Yes…"

"I'm going to use you, Katja," I warned her. "I'm going to use you until there's nothing left."

Her entire body shook with emotion. "Maksim…"

I pushed her face back down on the bed, and as she grabbed hold of the blanket again, I dropped another bead of spit onto her asshole, then slid my thumb inside. "Have you ever been fucked in the ass?"

"No…" she choked out brokenly.

My eyes almost crossed with her answer. "Never?"

"No…" she panted. "Never…"

"Then I guess I'll be the first to ever stretch it open," I smirked, my hips moving faster. "I wonder how much you'll be able to take your first time, baby."

"Oh, God…don't stop…" she cried out, the double penetration making her wild. "Maksim…please…"

"Are you going to cum for me?" I grunted, pushing into her deeper. "Are you going to cum all over my cock?"

"Yes…" she whimpered. "Don't stop…God, yes…"

When I removed my thumb, then replaced it with two other fingers, that's when Katja finally came for me, and her hold on my cock and fingers was tight enough to make me growl with the need to possess her forever. When I had suggested that she be my whore, I hadn't ever imagined that I'd want to keep her afterwards. However, there was no question about it now. No way would I ever let another man feel what I was feeling right now.

As soon as she was done cumming on my cock, I pulled my fingers out of her ass, then grabbed her by her hair again. Yanking her upward, I said, "I'm going to ruin you, Katja. I'm going to fuck you until you have to beg me to stop. I'm going to tear you apart, then put you back together just so that I can do it again."

"Maksim…" she whispered, her body cumming for me again.

Unable to stop myself, I let out a roar of my own as I finally came inside her, the condom a regret that I wasn't ever going to repeat again. My hips pushed up against her ass until I had nothing left to give, and even then, I didn't want to pull out of her. Still, never having been one to avoid reality, I knew that I needed to get her out of here and find a way to fix this. I knew without a doubt that Melor's phone was probably ringing off the hook with offers for Katja right now.

Pushing that thought from my mind, I pulled out of her, and the entire experience left me cold as her pussy clenched in the aftermath of her orgasm, my seed nowhere to be seen.

Yeah, that wasn't happening again.

# CHAPTER 18

*Katja ~*

My mind was a jumbled mess as I stared out the window, wondering what I was going to do. Things just kept getting more and more complicated, and if I were a stronger person, I'd be able to say that I hadn't been affected by what had happened between me and Maksim the other night. However, I'd been very affected, and as much as I hated it, I couldn't deny that it'd been the best sex of my life, despite how horrible the entire situation was.

When Maksim had finally slid inside me, everything had suddenly become primal and desperate, and I'd never felt that kind of need and hunger for a man before. His raspy voice had been like a hypnotizing symphony of dirty threats, and I had eaten it all up. His violent promises, his rough manhandling, his big dick doing damage...I'd been there for all of it, and my body still broke out in shivers whenever I remembered how it all felt.

There was also the way that he'd treated me afterwards. To my utter surprise and horror, Maksim had redressed me immediately after we'd been done, and I'd been terrified as I'd waited for him to tell me that I'd been horrible. However, instead, he had put me to rights, then had escorted us out of the room, driving me home himself. The entire thing had been awkward and uncomfortable, but I'd chosen to keep my mouth shut rather than borrow trouble.

When Maksim had finally dropped me off at home, he had walked me to my door, then had said that he'd call me later before leaving. It'd been our weirdest exchange to date, and I still didn't know what I was supposed to do with all of it because, three days later, I still hadn't heard from him.

"Think you can escape me that easily?"

I jumped in surprise as I turned to see Klive Simpson sitting down in the chair across from me. Even though I knew that his real name was Nikel, I just couldn't stop myself from thinking of him as Klive. I also hadn't expected for him to ambush me like this in public. Considering what was going on, I

71

thought that he'd want to stay as incognito as possible.

"What?"

His eyes looked dangerously alive with fire. "You think that I would not find out that you moved your grandfather, *milaya devushka?* Do you think that you are safe from me now?"

Doing my best to keep it together, I acted like the offended one. "Are you seriously upset with me because your plan is *working?*" I hissed. "Is that what's happening right now?"

His brows furrowed. "What are you speaking about?"

"I thought you *wanted* me to become Maksim's whore?" I bit out, making sure to keep my voice low. He'd found me eating lunch again, and Birdsoup's wasn't crowded enough to drown out our conversation. "I thought that you wanted me to get close to him, so that you could…what-the-hell-ever it is that you think?"

"What does that have to do with your grandfather living with you again?" he bit out, though making sure to keep his voice low, too.

"That first night that we were together, I tried to pillow-talk him like you wanted," I lied. "Well, since I don't have much of a life but wanted to sound sincere, I mentioned my grandfather. I mentioned how it bothered me that he couldn't be home with me, and…I don't know, Klive. I guess…I guess, instead of giving me diamonds or designer purses like a man would normally give to his mistress, he decided to pay for my grandfather's care at home."

"Really?" he deadpanned.

"I'm not lying," I hissed under my breath. "I was just as surprised as you are when I got the call that my grandfather was coming home. When I asked Maksim about it, he just ordered me to show my appreciation and that's all. How was I to know that he'd hire a live-in nurse?"

Klive leaned back in his chair. "Sounds like something the sonofabitch would do."

"Look, I have no idea what I'm doing here, so you need to cut me some fucking slack," I snapped. "I'm doing my best to get invited to his house, but until then, I don't know what you want from me."

"I want you to know that where your grandfather lays his head doesn't matter," he replied coldly. "Do you really believe that I cannot find my way into your home, *milaya devushka?*"

"Then what are you so pissed about?" I spat.

"Because I do not appreciate you not informing me of this change," he replied, and it had me wondering if all men with Barychev blood in their veins were straight crazy. Though I'd never met Akim Barychev, he was in the Russian bratva, so he had to be just as crazy as his brothers.

"And how in the hell was I supposed to do that?" I hissed. "Send a carrier pigeon?"

He shot me a look that reminded me of Maksim, but I didn't think that either man would appreciate the comparison. "Watch yourself, Katja

Volkov," he warned. "You are just lucky that I want Maksim more than I want to show you what I'm capable of."

Like a glass of cold water in my face, that brought me back to reality. While I knew enough of Maksim's reputation to be cautious of him, I knew nothing about Klive Simpson. For all that I knew, he could be more dangerous than Maksim, or Avgust Kotov for that matter.

Letting out a deep breath, I said, "Look, if you want regular updates, then you're going to have to find a way to contact me. If not, then I'm not sure what you want me to do."

"I have not survived this long by being stupid, *milaya devushka,*" he said. "If you've truly caught Maksim's attention, then he will take notice of another man being seen with you too often."

"Then what do you want me to do?" I asked, and it was a legitimate question this time.

Eyeing me, he finally said, "I will think on it, then let you know."

Still trying to prove that I was on his side, I asked, "What if I end up finding out something big?"

"I will find a solution to our problem soon," he replied evenly. "However, I must warn you, Katja. If you even *think* to betray me, I won't kill you. I'll keep you alive as I do the most unspeakable things to you, and if you think that I have a conscience, you would be wrong."

I was really getting tired of men threatening me, but I also knew that I couldn't do anything about it. At least, not without some realistic plan in place. However, there weren't any community college classes on how to deal with the Russian Bratva and their crazy relatives.

"Even with as much as I detest the position that you've put me in, I'm very much aware that you hold all the cards, Mr. Simpson," I said with enough disgust in my voice to make me sound genuine. "I wouldn't risk my grandfather's wellbeing for anything."

Klive eyed me for a long minute before finally saying, "There's one more thing."

My stomach tightened, but I did my best to appear confident. "What's that?"

"You've an incredible face and body, *milaya devushka,*" he said, making the air in my lungs freeze painfully. "I do not see why Maksim should be the only one able to enjoy it."

"Wh...what?" I asked, my mouth going dry.

"Why can you not be both our whore?" he asked as casually as if he were giving his food order. "You could let me know who the better lover is."

I started shaking my head. "I am not doing this," I insisted. "I've got Maksim believing that he is the only man that I am involved with. I am not going to risk my life for something that's not necessary to what you're trying to achieve."

"You think you can tell me no?" he asked, a sadistic smirk on his face.

"I'm telling you that the risk is too big," I said, praying for common sense to prevail. "I'm not that good of an actress, Mr. Simpson. I'm barely holding up under the strain as it is. If you decide to…to complicate things further, then you'll lose your chance at Maksim. If he finds out that I've lied to him about sleeping with other men, then you'll never get another woman close enough to him again." I let out a deep breath, my heart beating painfully against my ribs. "Don't let your hate for Maksim ruin the progress that we've made so far."

He arched a brow. "We've?"

"I've already proved that I'm willing to do anything to keep my grandfather safe," I told him. "So, yeah…*we've*. I have just as much invested in this as you do, if not more since I'm innocent in all this."

After a few seconds, he said, "Fine. We can hold off on that for now. However, once I've taken care of Maksim and Akim Barychev, I'm coming for your pussy, *milaya devushka*. I'm coming for it, and you'd better be ready."

He didn't say anything more as he got up from the chair, then walked out. It wasn't until the front door of the café shut behind him that I was finally able to breathe steadily. Now, while I didn't know what the exact rules were, I knew that I had to talk to Maksim. This was the third time that Klive had ambushed me out of the blue, the second time since we'd made our agreement. I didn't like continuously being caught unaware, and if Klive changed his mind about sleeping with me, then I had no idea what I was going to do.

Nevertheless, very aware that Klive might have eyes on me, I was going to wait until I got off work to text Maksim. He needed to know what was going on, and I wasn't too proud to admit that I needed some serious advice.

# CHAPTER 19

*Maksim ~*

When Katja had texted me that she needed to speak with me, I had immediately suspected the worst. However, she quickly regained my trust when she arranged for me to meet her at her work. Used to late-night emergencies, no one would think anything strange about reporting for work so late at night. Plus, with Artur now in charge of Mr. Antonov's care, Katja could come and go more freely.

So, after faking an emergency call, Katja went to the office to make it look like she was getting her necessary equipment, then she met me at one of our warehouses that was disguised as a legitimate business. I'd also had one of our kryshas meet her at the front door, taking the chance that Nikel wouldn't recognize him as one of ours. However, even if he did, it would make sense that I'd call my 'girlfriend' to help me out with some computer issues, considering what she did for a living.

Watching as Jurik walked out of the room, once he shut the door behind him, I turned to Katja pacing the floor, then asked, "What was so important, Katja?"

"Klive ambushed me again," she announced, making my back straighten. "He keeps doing that, and it's starting to worry me."

"When you say again, do you mean after the first time?"

Katja shook her head. "No. He ambushed me at work the other week, and then he ambushed me while I was eating lunch at Birdsoup."

"Are you fucking kidding me?" I snapped. "Why am I only hearing about this now?"

If looks could kill, then I'd be ash at her feet right now. "I don't exactly have permission to contact you, Maksim," she spat. "Plus, the last time that I saw you, I was too busy *auditioning* for you. I was more worried about keeping my grandfather alive than I was about Klive fucking Simpson."

"Watch yourself, *lyublyu,*" I warned. "I am not in the mood to be generous."

Her eyes glowed like fire. "Are you ever?"

"You're still alive, aren't you?" I pointed out coldly.

I watched her take in a deep breath, doing her best to remember who she was speaking to. "After I first met him, he pretended to make an appointment for IT services, then showed up at my work," she said, beginning to explain. He wanted to know what I'd learn so far, but I had pointed out that you'd hardly give up all your secrets after only one night together. He mentioned us being cozy at The Swan, which confirmed my suspicions that he would be watching me to see if I followed through. As proof, he wanted details...details of what happened in the restroom, so I told him."

"You told him that I fingered your cunt in the men's restroom?" I asked, surprised that she'd do such a thing. After all, it wouldn't show her in a favorable light.

She looked like she hated my guts. "I told him that I did my best to impress you, and that it must have worked because you asked for my number. He didn't ask for it, which surprised me, but I wasn't going to borrow trouble. Anyway, I asked him what his endgame was, and he said that he wanted to kill you and Akim without it costing him his own life. He said in order for him to be able to do that, he had to find a way in, and he thinks that if you're...enamored of me enough, then you'll eventually give me access to your home. If that happens, then I can tell him what I know, helping him get into your home, or office, or whatever. When I pointed out that your death would bring down the wrath of Avgust Kotov, he said that he welcomes it."

"What else?" I asked. "What did he want this second visit?"

I watched her drop back against the table behind her, and I could admit that she looked exhausted. Though always beautiful, she looked genuinely worn out.

Letting out another heavy sigh, she said, "He knows that my grandfather is living with me now, so he wanted to let me know that he could still get to him, no matter where he lived. He also didn't like how I hadn't told him about the move, and when I pointed out that I had no idea of how to get a hold of him, he didn't like that, either. He warned me not to betray him and-"

"Do not leave anything out, Katja," I said, reminding her that I was far more dangerous than Nikel.

She licked her lips before saying, "He said that I had an incredible face and body, and that he didn't see why he couldn't...why you were the only one that got to sleep with me." Rage licked at the back of my neck instantly. "He...he wanted me to compare you both to see who the better lover was."

"Katja, I will say this only once," I told her. "If you let that man touch you, I will kill you myself."

Her eyes widened in disbelief. "Because you actually think that I would *let* him touch me? Are you fucking serious right now?"

"What did you say to him?" I asked, ignoring her outrage.

She let out another deep breath, seemingly trying to calm herself down. "I told him that he'd be risking any progress that we've made. I told him that you'd know, and not only would you kill me, but you'd never trust another woman again. I...I told him not to allow his anger to cloud his judgement."

"Did it work?"

She nodded. "He said that he'd leave it alone for now. However, once he's taken care of you and Akim, he said that...that he's coming for my pussy, and that I'd better be ready. He also told me that if he finds out that I'm double-crossing him, instead of killing me, he's going to keep me alive and do unspeakable things to me."

Though I already had plans on tearing Nikel Ovchinnikov to pieces, now I was going to make him pay for tormenting Katja the way that he was. If he wanted a front-row seat to the unspeakable, then I was going to be glad to show him.

However, before I could let Katja know that, she asked, "How have you guys not caught him yet, Maksim? He knows enough of our whereabouts that he has to be following us, so why haven't your men picked up on a face that keeps appearing wherever you or your brother are?"

I did not like her insinuating that we were incompetent.

"Contrary to what you may have seen on television, but we've a multi-million-dollar empire to run, Katja," I told her. "We've an entire state that we operate in, and so we don't have a lot of available bodies to just keep their eyes to the streets. I also do not appreciate you implying that we're not doing our best to catch the sonofabitch, because we are."

"Well, then your best sucks," she spat, and I had my hand wrapped around her throat before she could even blink.

"Would you like to repeat that?" I asked, my voice deceptively low.

"No," she bit out through clenched teeth, remembering her place.

Letting go of her neck, I said, "You will meet me at The Swan again tomorrow night. However, before we get to that, I want to make sure that the man approaching you is really Nikel."

Her brows furrowed a bit, but she didn't say anything as I pulled out my phone, then showed her a snapshot of the picture that Morocco had managed to get for us. If he was wearing a disguise, then she'd be able to tell us, and it was stupid that I hadn't thought of it earlier. My only excuse was that she was affecting me more than was wise.

"That's him," she finally confirmed.

"So, he's not wearing a disguise when he visits you?"

She shook her head. "Not at all. Now, that's not to say that he's not wearing one when he's spying on you or us, but when he's ambushing me, he looks exactly like he does in that picture, only a bit older."

Putting my phone away, I said, "You will meet me at nine o'clock at The Swan. From there, you'll accompany me to my home. If Nikel is watching as we all suspect, then he'll know that I am taking you to my place. He'll think that his plan is working, and I'm willing to bet that he'll probably approach you again the next day to satisfy his curiosity."

"Fine," she sighed tiredly. "Whatever you say, Maksim."

I took her chin in my fingers. "Nothing has changed between us, Katja. You will continue to spread your legs for me, no matter how angry at me you are. There is no way out of this for you, except for one, and that choice will leave your grandfather with no one."

Katja jerked her face from my hold. "You can save your threats, Maksim. I haven't forgotten my role in all of this."

"*Lyublyu,* you really need to learn how to control that temper of yours," I said, quietly reprimanding her. "I've little patience as it is. My graciousness will run out sooner or later."

Ignoring that, she asked, "Are we done here? I'm tired and want to go home."

"I will see you tomorrow night," I told her, refusing to give her attitude any credit. "Wear something that is designed to drive a man out of his mind."

"Of course," she bit out before turning to leave, and I let her go, giving Jurik the nod to follow her out to her car. While I did not like her driving around at night by herself, I had to remind myself that that was part of her job, and if I wanted to keep her, then I was going to have to find a way to make that work.

Saving my issues with Katja for another time, I pulled out my phone, then dialed Avgust to let him know what was going on, and that I was going to absolutely destroy Nikel once I got my hands on him.

# CHAPTER 20

*Katja ~*

I walked into The Swan, and I felt like all eyes were on me, though that wasn't true. However, now that I'd actually had sex with Maksim, I was officially a whore for the Russian Bratva, even if I was only laying down for Maksim right now. Like Klive, I had no idea what more would be asked for me at a later date, and I'd have to be super stupid to believe that Maksim might see me as something more than a means to an end.

At any rate, unlike last time, he hadn't escorted me inside, and for whatever reason, it felt like déjà vu of the first time that I had walked in here. Honestly, I didn't know which was worse, not knowing what I'd been getting myself into or knowing exactly what Maksim expected of me now.

It also didn't help that I actually felt something inexplicable for Maksim Barychev. While it was rather sick and twisted if you thought about it, I couldn't get the other night out of my mind, no matter how hard I tried. I'd never cum so hard in my life, and it was shameful to admit that I wanted him to do it again. I wasn't sure what that made me, but I knew enough to know that it didn't make me a good person; a good person would have gone to the police. Or maybe that was a smart person. A smart person would have gone to the police, and then allowed the wheels of justice to do their thing. Now I was embroiled in a mess that had me way deep in over my head.

As soon as I stepped up near the bar, I looked around the room until I saw Maksim seated in a corner booth. He lifted his tumbler of liquor in my direction, and I almost laughed like an idiot. I had no idea if he was just flagging me down, or if he expected me to get him another drink. A second later, I felt like crying. I felt like everything around me was falling apart, and no matter how hard I tried, I didn't have enough strength to hold any of it up.

Figuring that it was a whore's job to service her keeper in all areas, I turned to the bar, then signaled for the bartender. When she walked over, I asked, "Can I get a...Maksim Barychev needs another drink."

Dropping everything, she quickly made his drink, and not wanting to offend her or Maksim, I held my tongue when she told me how much it cost. Thankfully, I'd had enough sense to put some cash in my purse before coming out tonight, so I slid her a hundred-dollar bill, then told her to keep the change. I felt stupid because she probably expected more, but I didn't have much more to give her.

Doing my best to shake off my nerves, I grabbed Maksim's drink, then turned to head towards his booth. Walking over, I was careful not to spill any of the expensive vodka because I couldn't afford to get him another one right now. Granted, I could always use my ATM card, but I'd rather pay cash at places like this. It was an expensive slippery slope to start putting drinks on a tab.

When I finally reached the table, I placed the glass in front of him, and it wasn't until I got comfortable in the booth that I notice how wild his eyes looked. "Is...is everything okay?"

"Did you just buy me a drink?" he asked, and his voice held a touch of that familiar darkness that I was beginning to recognize. Maksim was pissed, only I had no idea why.

"Uh...yes," I stammered. "I...I thought that's what you wanted when you lifted your glass."

Maksim's fingers grabbed me by my chin before squeezing painfully enough to get my attention. "Do not ever spend your own money on me, Katja," he ordered. "Do you understand?"

"It's...it's just a drink," I replied, resenting how he was making me feel stupid for doing something so simple.

"*I* support *you*," he practically snarled. "You *do not* support me, understand? Do not ever do something like that again."

I could only stare at him.

*What in the fresh hell?*

Before I could say anything to that, Maksim let go of my chin, then got up from the booth. I watched as he stormed across the room towards the bar, then tell the bartender that had helped me something unpleasant. She looked like she was facing the firing squad, and I immediately felt bad for placing her in Maksim Barychev's crosshairs.

When Maksim finally returned to the booth, he pulled out his wallet, and I watched in stunned silence as he pulled out a hundred-dollar bill, then drop it on the table in front of me. I stared at it like it was a snake, ready to bite me, but I didn't know why. For some reason, this moment felt significant, but this was also just another game with no real rules. It was just a drink, but Maksim was acting as if I'd insulted his mother.

"Take it and place it back in your wallet," he ordered. "Now, Katja. Do it now before I really lose my shit."

Not wanting to cause a scene, I quickly did as he'd demanded, regretting not getting a drink for myself. I was also so damn sick of this shit.

"It was just a drink," I repeated.

Ignoring that, he finally took a seat next to me, asking, "What is wrong? You seem upset."

I looked over at him, my eyes wide. "Are you serious? *Everything* is wrong, Maksim. With the exception of my grandfather finally coming home, everything about these past couple of weeks is wrong. I mean, what is there that's right?"

"Have you forgotten the other night already?" he asked, his voice low, and I hated how that simple question had my body clenching.

"Maksim-"

His hand on my bare thigh immediately shut me up, and I stared into his chocolate-colored gaze unbelievingly as his palm trailed up the inside of my leg, the man not caring that we were out in public. Though I couldn't deny the dark shiver of need that raced down my spine, I'd also never been this adventurous. I'd never been a big public-displays-of-affection kind of person, and I'd definitely never been the type of person to have sex in public.

When Maksim's fingers reached the apex of my thighs, he said, "Let me help you forget your troubles, *lyublyu.*"

I could barely speak as his fingers slid inside my panties. "Maksim, we're...we're in pub...public."

"Do you think that anyone is going to comment?" he asked, his voice a dark symphony of need.

It was on the tip of my tongue to tell him that I wasn't a whore, but the words wouldn't come out. After all, that's exactly what I was, and I needed to stop living in a time before Klive Simpson had entered my life; I was no longer that woman. Besides, sex in public didn't automatically make a woman a whore. Lots of couples found the risqué behavior sexy and empowering. I mean, what was hotter than someone wanting you so badly that they were unable to wait until they got you home?

So, with nothing significant to say, I just stared into his dark gaze as his fingers worked their way inside me, the stretch eliciting a shameful moan from my lips. When the slick sounds of his ministrations hit my ears, I curled my fingers around the edge of the seat, the soft fabric tightening in my grip. It felt both embarrassing and exhilarating to be doing this, but I also wasn't going to stop him. Even if I could, my body didn't want him to stop. Everything that Maksim Barychev did felt like sin wrapped up in more sin, and every inch of me enjoyed it all.

With no choice but to just hang on for the ride, I licked my lips, then closed my eyes, and that's when Maksim abruptly pulled his fingers from my pussy.

When my eyes snapped open, he said, "I've decided that this does not work for me."

*He was cancelling our arrangement.*

I didn't say anything as he dropped another large bill on the table, then stood up, leaving his fresh drink untouched. When he walked around to stand in front of me, he reached down, and on autopilot, I grabbed his hand, then allowed him to help me stand as I quickly grabbed my purse.

As Maksim escorted me out of The Swan, my mind began to race with what I was going to do now. Waves of rage also coursed through my body as I realized just how sinister Maksim Barychev really was. Like a sadistic sonofabitch, he'd waited until my grandfather was back home before pulling the rug back out from under me. He'd waited until I'd felt that familiar sense of comfort before finally making me pay for ever agreeing to help Klive. Everything made sense now. It explained why he hadn't waited for me outside like he'd done before.

Since Maksim's car had remained out front, just right across the street, as soon as Jurik saw us walking toward the vehicle, he walked over, then immediately opened the door to the backseat. With his hand on the small of my back, Maksim escorted me inside, then said something to Jurik in Russian before getting inside the car himself.

Once we were on our way, I stared at my hands in my lap as my heartbeat drummed in my ears. Everything was spinning so out of control, and I really felt like I was losing my mind. I had no idea if Maksim was taking me home or taking me out into the country to shoot me dead, and I almost laughed with the absurdity of it all. However, before I could become completely hysterical, Maksim Barychev was surprising me once again.

"Now let's finished what we started, *lyublyu.*"

# CHAPTER 21

*Maksim ~*

"Wh…what?" Katja stammered as she looked over at me, her eyes wide.

Since I hadn't bothered to put on my seatbelt, it was easy to turn in my seat. "I said that we can now finish what we started earlier."

Her amber-colored gaze glanced over towards the back of Jurik's head. "But-"

"He has his earbuds in and knows better than to look back here," I reassured her. "It'll be his life if he doesn't keep his eyes on the road, and he knows it."

"Maksim-"

"Come over here, Katja," I ordered. "Come straddle my lap, baby."

Though still shooting glances Jurik's way, Katja unbuckled her seatbelt, then climbed over my lap. As soon as she was straddling my hard dick, I grabbed the strap of her dress, then pulled it down her arm until her left breast bounced free. Finally able to do all the things that I hadn't been able to that first time, I leaned forward, then took her hardened peak into my mouth, and she tasted as pure as the driven snow; no lotions or perfumes to compromise my taste buds.

"Maksim…" she moaned, no longer worried about Jurik.

My left hand reached up to knead her right breast through the fabric of her dress, and I couldn't wait to get her home. I wanted her completely naked, laid out for me to do whatever I wished. I wanted to lick every inch of her skin, and I wanted her stunning body on display as I did it. I wanted to study her like the piece of priceless art that she was.

When Katja's hips started moving across my groin, I reached up to grab the back of her hair, and when I yanked her head back, my lips traveled up her neck, and I did something that I'd never done before; I marked her for all the world to see. I also wasn't going to stop at just one. I was going to leave proof of what we had all over her precious body.

There was also the fact that Melor had called me the morning after I'd taken Katja in the showroom. He'd call to inform me that Jewelle had phoned him to tell him that all anyone could talk about was Katja and our performance the other night. According to Melor, the bid to be her first was already in the tens of thousands, and Katja could easily pay for her grandfather's care and then some if I was stupid enough to allow it. Despite my original plan to give Katja an option when this was all said and done, the more of her that I tasted, the more addicted I became.

The second that I was done leaving my mark on her, my mouth went back to devouring her tit, and when she let out another moan, her fingers began digging into my shoulders. Katja was so responsive that I mentally urged Jurik to drive fucking faster. For the first time in my life, I wanted a woman in my bed, and I felt as eager as a school-aged boy.

Needing more, I slid one hand underneath the bunched-up fabric of her dress, then wasted no time slipping it between her legs. Katja was still wet from earlier, and the slick sounds were like music to my ears because they mattered. Considering how we'd met and what had been demanded of her, the fact that she could still find pleasure in my touch mattered.

"I love how wet you get for me, baby," I told her, my lips still pressed against her skin, her nipple still in my mouth. "Your pussy is always so ready for my cock."

"Maksim…" she whimpered. "Don't stop…"

As two of my fingers found their way into her tight pussy, I asked, "What, *lyublyu?* Tell me what you need."

"Make me cum…" she ordered shamelessly. "Maksim…please…"

With my two fingers inside her soaked cunt, I used my thumb to play with that little button of hers, and it wasn't long before she was arching her back, panting uncontrollably. Katja really was a stunning vision when she was cumming for me, and it was something that I wouldn't mind experiencing for a very long time to come.

"Christ, you're beautiful," I told her, her pussy clamping down hard on my fingers, her orgasm shaking her entire body. "So fucking beautiful."

When Katja was finally done with her trip to paradise, I pulled my fingers out of her cunt, then licked them clean, not wanting to wait until I got her home to properly eat her pussy. There was so much that I wanted to do to her, and Jurik just wasn't driving fast enough.

Quietly, I went to fixing her dress, and that's when she finally opened her eyes to look at me. She looked like she wanted to say so much, but whatever was happening between us, now was not the time.

"Is that your favorite thing to do?" she asked in a soft voice, surprising me.

"What?"

Her eyes shifted a bit before saying, "Uhm…putting your hand between my thighs? You've done it since that first night."

Looking into her sun-colored eyes, I said, *"You* are my favorite thing to do. It doesn't matter what we're doing or where I'm touching you. I enjoy it all."

She gave me a small nod before moving to get off my lap, and I let her. There was something heavy in the air, and I knew what it was, even if she didn't. Katja had begun to matter to me, yet I kept using her like a whore, and that was a problem. While I could excuse my actions by admitting that it was hard for me to keep my hands off her when she was around, that wouldn't be a good enough excuse for someone like her. Katja had led a simple life, and though it'd been Nikel that had disrupted it, I hadn't helped by forcing her into all this, and I knew that I needed to rethink my strategy to draw Nikel out in the open. Every day that I let her live her life in peace, she was in danger, and I knew that I was going to need to speak to Avgust about other options.

Nothing more was said between us until Jurik pulled into the underground garage. While I had a secluded home in the country, I had a penthouse in town for practical reasons. Now, while the house in the country was my primary residence, Katja was still the first and only woman that I'd ever brought here. Though a part of me wanted her in my home, another part needed to test her if I really planned on making something more of this fucked-up situation.

"Where are we?" she asked, looking around.

"My home," I answered simply.

Katja's head whipped my way, her eyes wide. "What are we doing here?"

I arched a brow as I turned slightly to get a good look at her. "What do you think? I've the need for you, and I need a bed for all the things that I want to do to you."

"Why can't we go to a hotel room for that?" she asked, a bit of alarm in her voice. "We don't..." She began shaking her head as she took in a deep breath. "I don't want to be here, Maksim. I don't want to know where you live."

I cocked my head a bit. "Why not?"

"Nothing good can come of me knowing where you live," she rushed out. "I have no idea what future plans Klive has for me, and I don't want to know anything that he might be able to...to..."

"Finish," I instructed.

"If he ends up torturing me, I can't say that I'll be strong enough to withstand it, so I'd rather know nothing," she confessed honestly as she started shaking her head again. "I don't want to be here. Let's go somewhere else."

"I want you in *my* bed, Katja," I told her, ignoring her admission. "I am not interested in hotel sheets smelling like you in the morning."

Her eyes immediately started to water. "I don't want to be here, Maksim," she repeated. "Please don't do this to me."

"It's too late, *lyublyu,"* I informed her, breaking the news to her. "You've already seen where I live."

A lone tear escaped, but she quickly brushed it away. She also didn't say anything more as Jurik pulled into my parking spot, but what would be the point? Katja was a smart girl, and she could see the writing on the wall just as everyone else. I was calling the shots here, despite how Nikel believed that he was the one in charge.

Once the car was in park, I got out, then rounded the back of the vehicle to open Katja's door. However, I had barely cleared the back end before I heard her car door open, and by the time that I reached her, she was already shutting the door.

*That pissed me off.*

"Do not ever do that again," I ordered.

Katja blinked at me. "Do what?"

"Open your own door," I clarified. "You wait until it is opened for you."

"Why?" She genuinely looked baffled.

"Because that is what's proper," I answered simply.

Her brows shot upward, but she didn't say anything more. She didn't agree or disagree, but just walked with me towards the elevators, and I knew that it was going to be a long night.

# CHAPTER 22

*Katja ~*

I had no idea what was going on with Maksim, but the man was giving me whiplash. Who in the hell treated their whore *properly?* What kind of nonsense was that?

Nevertheless, my stomach felt like it was tied in knots as I watched Maksim unlock his front door, and I'd never wanted to *not* be somewhere so badly in all my life. I hadn't been lying when I'd said that I didn't want to know where Maksim lived. I didn't want to know anything about him because then it'd feel too much like I was doing as Klive had demanded of me, and I wasn't.

As soon as Maksim unlocked the door, he placed his hand on the small of my back, then ushered me inside. Once the door was shut behind us, I turned to face the bratva leader, and he was looking at me in a way that just made me more confused. Considering how we'd met and what we were doing, I shouldn't be here, and I couldn't understand why he couldn't see that.

"I really don't want to be here," I told him again. "Why can't we go to a hotel?"

"I already told you," he replied evenly. "I'm not concerned with random hotel sheets smelling like you."

"That makes no sense," I sighed, beginning to feel frustrated. "Just like opening my door. Since when does a man have to treat a whore with manners? That's absurd."

Maksim stepped towards me and didn't stop until he was standing directly in front of me. "Do not ever call yourself that again."

*Now I was really freakin' confused.*

"What?"

"You heard me," he said, his voice carrying a bit of an edge. "You will not refer to yourself as that again."

"Why not?" I asked stubbornly. "It's what we agreed to, Maksim. It's the

87

very reason that I'm even here."

He grabbed my chin in his fingers, forcing my head up. "Is it?" he asked challengingly. "Are you telling me that you're not attracted to me, Katja? Are you telling me that you feel nothing for me whenever I have my hands on you? Are you really just here to play your part as my whore?"

Maksim was pissing me off.

He wasn't playing fair.

This wasn't part of the deal.

"That's not fair, and you know it," I practically spat. "Quit trying to manipulate me when it's not necessary, Maksim. I'm here. I'm doing what you ordered me to do. I'm doing my best to help you find Klive while not getting my grandfather and myself killed. What fucking more do you want from me?"

"Watch how you speak to me, *lyublyu,*" he warned as he let go of my chin.

I let out a dark laugh. "Or else what? You're going to kill me?" I was losing it, but I didn't care. "Then do it, because I'm really fucking tired of this shit. I have you threatening to kill me, and Klive threatening to rape me before he kills me, but not before I also get to watch him kill my grandfather." I tiredly shook my head. "Christ, are you men good for anything else?"

"Oh, I can show you lots of other things that I am good for," he snapped before wrapping his hand around my neck, then dragging me through his penthouse.

Once we got to his bedroom, he was none too gentle when he tossed me on the bed, and before I could even get comfortable, Maksim grabbed my thighs, then pulled my ass to the edge of the bed. I gasped when he got on his knees, then flung my legs over his shoulders, and my fingers fisted in the sheets as soon as I heard the tearing of my panties.

*Holy shit.*

Common sense immediately fled the second that I felt the first swipe of Maksim's tongue through my pussy lips, and I let out a moan that had me wanting to crawl into a hole and never come out. I had just lectured him on all the ways that my life was fucked-up, and he was just making it worse by reminding me that my pride was worthless in this situation. He'd asked me if I felt anything when he was touching me, and my soaked center was proof enough that I did. Even when he was manhandling me, I was still turned on, and if that didn't make me officially crazy, then I didn't know what did.

When Maksim pulled his mouth off my pussy, it was only to slide two fingers inside me and say, "For only you, I'd ever get on my knees like this." I didn't know what that meant, but I also didn't have the sense right now to ask him to explain. "Your pussy tastes divine, Katja."

"Maksim…" I whimpered as his mouth landed back on my clit, his tongue manipulating it expertly.

I wasn't sure how long I just laid there and let him have his way with me, but when a third finger slid carefully into my ass, all I could do was grip the sheets tighter. I'd never had a man do that before, and fire licked up my spine at how good it felt. In fact, it felt so good that I'd never judge a threesome ever again. Maksim penetrating both my holes felt like a decadent evil that I could easily become addicted to.

This was also vastly different than from when he'd done it the other night. The other night, he'd been fucking me, shoving his fingers inside my ass to prove a point. However, that wasn't what was happening right now. Instead of showing me who was in charge, Maksim was using everything that he had to drive me out of my mind with pleasure, and it was working. With his fingers, lips, and tongue all working together, there probably wasn't anything that I wouldn't let this man do to me.

"Maksim...don't stop..." I begged, already nearing the edge. "Please..."

When Maksim took that to mean more, he slipped another finger inside my ass, and that was all it took for me to explode all over the place. Letting go of the sheets, I grabbed onto his dark hair, then rode his face with no shame, and his deep growls only encouraged me more. I no longer cared if this was right or wrong, and however this ended, I was never going to forget these moments. No matter what, this level of pleasure was going to stay with me forever.

*Or for however long I lived.*

My eyes finally opened when I felt Maksim remove my legs from his shoulders, and when I looked up, he was already standing, removing his clothes with the grace of a wild jungle cat, and in this moment, the answer to all his questions was no. I did feel something for him, and despite how much I shouldn't, I couldn't stop myself from caring about the man the more time that I spent with him. I'd officially lost my mind, and I had no idea how to come back from the loss.

I watched silently as Maksim removed his guns, placed them on the floor, then finished getting undress. Once he was completely naked, my heart started hammering inside my chest, his dark gaze warning me that he wasn't going to take it easy on me tonight. Whatever Maksim had planned, it was going to change me forever, and I wasn't even sure if I wanted to stop him.

As I went to move up higher on the bed, Maksim stopped me by grabbing the neckline of my dress, then yanking on it hard enough to rip down the middle. Since I didn't have any extra clothes with me, I wasn't sure how he was going to send me home, but I'd worry about that later. Right now, Maksim looked like he wanted to eat me alive, so maybe there wasn't going to be anything left of me by the time he was done.

I didn't say anything as he crawled over my body, this feeling completely different from the other night, but when he flipped us over, I gasped. I was straddling his hard dick, and I seriously doubted if I was going to be able to take him like this; Maksim Barychev was simply too big.

"You're going to ride my cock while those tits of yours bounce in my face, baby," he ordered. "You're going to fuck yourself on my dick until you flood the fucking bed."

With my hands planted on his chest, my eyes on his, I said, "You forgot the condom."

With one hand planted firmly on my hip, Maksim used his other one to reach up, grab a fistful of my hair, then pulled me against him until our noses were practically touching. "No, I didn't," he replied, his raspy voice sounding like he wanted to murder me right here.

"Maksim-"

"I'm cumming inside you, Katja," he informed me, not even asking me if it was okay. "You are mine, and because you are mine, I get to flood your womb whenever the fuck I want. Because you are mine, I do not need to use a condom. Because you are mine, I am free to do with you as I please."

As absurd as his declarations were, I had to tell him the truth. "If I get pregnant, I will not have an abortion, Maksim. I won't...that's not an acceptable form of birth control for me."

His hand went from my hair to circling my neck, then squeezing tightly. "If you ever end up pregnant with my child, I will kill you with my bare hands if you even think to rid yourself of it."

Not having any damn idea what was going on, I asked, "What are you doing, Maksim? What is this?"

Though he didn't let go of my neck, he did quit squeezing it. "This is me and you, Katja. That's what this is."

The next thing that I knew, Maksim had a hold of my hips, holding me still as he slammed his hard length into me from underneath, and all I could do was hold on, my screams echoing throughout the room, Maksim refusing to let me go until I begged him hours later.

# CHAPTER 23

*Maksim ~*

"I'm here," Avgust announced. "What is the emergency?"

After Katja had finally tapped out last night, I had texted Avgust, requesting a meeting with him first thing this morning. We needed a new plan because Katja simply wasn't an option anymore. Now, while I knew that it was going to take some convincing, she didn't really have any choice, and neither did her grandfather. I planned on speaking with him soon, but he was going to eventually learn that his granddaughter was going to marry into the Russian Bratva, and he was just going to have to deal with it.

"It is hardly an emergency," I drawled out.

"You have summoned me at all hours of the morning, Maksim," he said like an asshole. "How can it not be an emergency?"

I slid a coffee mug his way. "It is not my fault that becoming a father has turned you into an old man," I retorted.

Avgust grinned as he took a seat at my kitchen table, grabbing the mug as he did so. "I wouldn't have it any other way," he replied happily, and I believed him.

Getting to the reason why I had called him here, I said, "We need to come up with another plan to drawl Nikel out in the open."

Avgust's brows shot upward. "We do?"

"Katja's asleep in my bed right now," I informed him, telling him everything that he needed to know with that one sentence.

"Well, that escalated quickly," he smirked before taking a sip of his plain coffee.

"I cannot have her unprotected anymore," I told him, ignoring his quip.

"While I completely understand where you are coming from, as long as Nikel doesn't know that she is double-crossing him, she should be safe, no?"

"Yes," I agreed. "However, I no longer want her away from my bed."

Avgust's hazel eyes narrowed in thought. "Which would play exactly into

91

Nikel's plans, no?"

"While it would, I no longer appreciate the risk now that he's made his intentions with Katja clear," I replied evenly, doing my best to keep my emotions out of this conversation. Avgust was here as my Pakhan, not my friend.

"Everything that we know is still not good enough," he remarked evenly.

As my Pakhan, Avgust knew everything that I did. He knew about her conversations with Klive, the showroom, and that her grandfather was now home. There wasn't anything that Avgust didn't know about this situation, though we were still trying our best to keep Akim out of this. My brother knew only what he had to know in order to keep his family safe.

"I'm willing to pay the Sartoris," I finally told him.

His head jerked in surprise. "Pay them for what?"

"Morocco, of course," I answered. "While Katja confirmed that Nikel is the same man in our pictures, he obviously has to be in disguise when he's stalking me or Akim. He knew that I was at The Swan that first night, and he also knows too much about Katja's movements. If we can get Morocco to pull security footage from the neighboring cameras from everywhere that Katja and I have been these past few weeks, then we can compare faces in the background. Hell, if he can just pull the feed from either Trevally's or Birdsoup, we can see a more updated version of his face."

Eyeing me, Avgust asked, "What are your intentions with her, Maksim?"

"I am going to marry her," I answered honestly.

"And does she know this?" he asked, chuckling under his breath like an asshole.

"Not as of yet," I told him. "However, after everything that I just did to her last night, she should have an idea."

Not surprised by the choices that I made in life, Avgust said, "As much as I applaud you conquering your fears of commitment, she is believed to be for sale, Maksim. Are you certain that she's willing to choose marriage to you over all the money that she could be making when this is all over?"

"She doesn't know," I admitted.

Avgust scowled. "What doesn't she know?"

"She is unaware of why we had sex at Millie's," I clarified. "She's under the impression that it was just another hotel room of sorts."

"*Iisus Khristos,*" he swore as he ran a hand through his dark hair.

"It is something that cannot be undone, Avgust," I pointed out.

"Maksim, you are going to lose her when she finds out what you've done," he said, and I knew that he was speaking to me as my friend right now. "While it can't be undone, something needs to be done to salvage this situation."

"I plan on telling her the truth soon," I told him.

I watched Avgust let out a deep sigh. "There is no way to clean this up without further humiliating her, Maksim. If you do nothing, then everyone will believe that you married a whore. If you say that it was merely a…a fantasy that you were fulfilling for your girlfriend, then men will believe that she enjoys being leered at. No matter what path you choose, she will still end up the loser in all this."

"I'll simply say that I enjoy showing her off," I semi-lied. While I did enjoy having her on my arm, that was different from parading her modesty around to one and all.

"I will call Nero," Avgust announced, surprising me.

"You will?"

He nodded. "The sooner that we capture Nikel, the sooner that we can spread the word that Katja's little act was for the betterment of the bratva. We can let it be known that she is not-*nor was she ever*-a whore, and that she had agreed to do what she did to help us set a trap." He shook his head as his mind raced with the best way to help me on this. "The story is believable if we spin it correctly."

"It could work," I muttered, wondering why I hadn't thought of it first. Of course, my emotions were involved, so that changed things a bit.

Avgust eyed me again. "You need to tell her the truth soon, Maksim," he advised. "I'll let Melor know that she is unavailable and to begin fielding calls, but since the word is already out there, it's possible that she might hear it from someone else."

"She is around no bratva unless she is with me," I reminded him. "The rest of the time, she is at work or at home with her grandfather."

"Maksim, I am telling you this as your friend," he said seriously. "Tell her before she finds out from someone else. Being honest with her will be the difference between getting yourself a wife or a prisoner. Trust me on this."

"There's only one little problem with telling her now, Pakhan," I replied.

"And what would that problem be?"

"Right now, she is honoring her word to help us lure Nikel out in the open. If I tell her what I did to her, what guarantee do I have that she won't flip on us?" I posed. "A woman scorned is one that does not care about any consequences to her wrath, something that we both are very aware of."

After mulling my words over for a bit, he finally said, "Let me call Nero. That's our best course of action right now."

I gave him a terse nod. "Let him know that I am willing to pay whatever price tag that he feels appropriate."

With the rest of his coffee untouched, Avgust stood up to leave. "Is there anything else that I can help you with?"

"Katja needs some clothes," I told him. "I cannot send her home in my stuff, but I also cannot send her home naked. Her grandfather might have an issue with that."

Ignoring the part about Katja's grandfather, Avgust asked, "And what are you going to do about her job? I imagine that she'll no longer be allowed to work, no?"

I ran a hand through my hair. "Once we're married, she'll understand why I cannot have her working."

"You're putting a lot of faith in that little piece of paper, Maksim," he remarked dryly.

"Just call Nero," I said. "I'll deal with the rest of it once Nikel Ovchinnikov is no longer an issue."

Avgust smirked. "Good luck. I am fairly certain that you are going to need it, *bratok*."

"Thanks," I replied wryly.

"I will ask Samara to pick out a few things, then have them delivered downstairs," he said, finally addressing the issue of Katja's lack of clothing. "Send me a picture of the clothes that you ruined, so that we have an idea of her size."

"Sure thing," I replied, grateful that he was doing this for me.

Not needing me to host him, Avgust showed himself out of my penthouse, leaving me with a fucking headache. Though I'd already known that this thing with Katja was going to be hard to navigate, a woman scorned really was the most frightening thing on earth.

# CHAPTER 24

*Katja ~*

While I was doing my best to concentrate on living a normal life, it wasn't easy. After Maksim had used me the other night, I had convinced him to give me a few days to get some air, and luckily for me, he had agreed. While we might be playing right into what Klive had been hoping for, I had explained how I couldn't keep disappearing at night without my grandfather getting suspicious, and so Maksim had agreed to give me a few days to live my life normally, though he'd made it clear that it would be a small reprieve and nothing more.

At any rate, while my grandfather and Artur seemed to be settling in nicely, I felt like I was going crazy, and the regular banality of work was actually the only thing that felt comforting. When I was at work, I didn't feel as if my life was falling apart. When I was at work, I didn't have crazy Russians threatening to kill me and my grandfather. When I was at work, I didn't have a high-ranking member of the Russian Bratva hypnotizing me with things that were impossible. When I was at work, I was simply Katja Volkov, IT tech.

Nonetheless, as crazy as I felt, I wasn't a complete fool. Letting Maksim go without protection the other night had been the worst thing that I could possibly do, and that was saying something, considering everything that I'd been through these past few weeks. While I had every confidence in my birth control, nothing was guaranteed, so using condoms only bettered the odds against an unplanned pregnancy. After all, the last thing that I needed was to get pregnant by Maksim freakin' Barychev. Though he'd made some very cryptic statements the other night, I'd been too tired and lost in his touch to demand further explanation. Like a coward, I'd stuck my head in the sand, then had left it there until Maksim had delivered me safely to my front door the next morning.

Unfortunately, I wasn't going to be able to play blind for much longer.

Things were becoming complicated, and my feelings for Maksim were at the center of all the complications. I was never supposed to have fallen for the man, but I'd had. Like a fucking idiot, I'd had, and now I had no idea what I was supposed to do.

"Oh, it *is* you."

I turned to see a woman pulling her grocery cart up next to mine. "Excuse me?"

"It's your eyes," she said, further confusing me. "They're kind of hard to miss."

My brows furrowed. "Do I know you?"

Admittedly, I came across a lot of people in my field of work, but this woman was pretty enough to be rememberable. She was shorter than I was, putting her at around five-foot-one, had silky brown hair, dark eyes, and she was petite enough to feed every stereotype about delicate Asian women. She was truly an exotic beauty, so I was pretty sure that I would have remembered if we'd met before.

"Well, no," she answered, pushing her cart closer, putting us right in front of each other. "We weren't able to meet that night."

The hairs on the back of my neck immediately stood up. "What night? What are you talking about?"

She leaned in conspiratorially, then lowered her voice to a whisper. "The night at Millie's."

Dread started forming in the pit of my stomach. The night at Millie's, neither Maksim nor I had spoken to anyone. As soon as I had arrived, he'd taken me straight to the suite, and we had left immediately after he'd been done with me. Neither of us had socialized with anyone, and I honestly couldn't remember seeing this woman there. Granted, I hadn't been looking to make any new friends, but I would have remembered seeing her there; I was sure of it. Plus, why would we have needed to meet each other?

"I'm sorry," I said, trying to keep my voice steady. "I…I don't remember seeing you there."

"Well, considering that you were only there for the showing, I'm not surprised," she replied. "Not to mention that you had Maksim Barychev showing you off."

Even though I had no idea what she was talking about, I didn't want her to know that. It was obvious that she knew something that I didn't, and I needed all the information that I could get if I was going to be able to navigate through all this shit and still remain alive.

"Does…does Maksim not do that often?" I asked, my stomach already tied in knots.

"No," she answered. "As you probably already know, Melor Kotov oversees the bratva whores, and before he got married, he used to break us in every once in a while, but never Maksim. In fact, it's usually the guards or street soldiers that break in the whores."

*What in the fuck?*

"Who...uhm, who gets to decide?" I asked. "I mean, I can only imagine how many men sign up for the privilege, right?"

She laughed, and it sounded like a lullaby. "It depends on the girl," she answered. "And considering how beautiful you are, I can see why Maksim insisted on breaking you in himself."

"How...how long have you...you worked for the Kotovs?" I asked, my heartbeat drumming in my ears.

"About four years already." She shrugged a shoulder. "Before that, I was on my own in the streets, so working for the Kotovs is so much better. However, because I'd already been...*seasoned*, there'd been no need to present me in the showcase room."

"The showcase room?" I echoed.

She nodded. "Yeah, where you and Maksim had sex." I felt like I was going to throw up, but before I could, she kept prattling on. "I saw you guys walk in, but when Maksim flipped the switch to inform the patrons that a new whore was being showcased, the guy that I was with that night had wanted to see the new merchandise." She shrugged like it didn't bother her, and maybe it didn't. "So, we were able to procure one of the rooms, and when Maksim hit the switch to lift the curtains, the second that my date saw you, he was already informing me how much he was willing to pay to see us together."

"I...I must have gotten turned around, because...I didn't see anyone," I semi-lied.

The girl rolled her eyes. "You mean that Maksim didn't tell you how it worked?"

I shook my head. "He just said that I needed to audition for him."

"The walls to that room are two-way mirrors," she announced, and it took everything that I had in me not to throw up everywhere. "It's surrounded by eight individual rooms that patrons can rent to watch the show. They see what's available, then put in their bids." She leaned in a little bit closer, like we were best friends that were sharing secrets. "Last I heard, the bid to be your first is at twenty-thousand dollars."

"What?" I choked out.

She nodded. "With the bratva taking twenty percent, that's still a good chunk of change. Plus, the fact that Maksim Barychev was the one that broke you in upped your value considerably. If you can take a dick that size, then there probably isn't much you can't handle. There's also the fact that everyone heard how you're an anal virgin, so the men are probably climbing the castle gates to get to you."

It was hard to speak, but I managed. "What's your...your name?"

"Oh," she grinned as she stuck her hand out to shake mine. "Janet. Janet Woo."

I shook her hand. "I'm Katja Volkov."

"You know, it's none of my business, but I can't help but wonder how you got mixed up with Maksim," she said. "You don't seem like the...like one of us."

Sticking to the truth as much as possible, I said, "I have debt."

She gave me a small nod of her head. "Well, I'll be at Erato's this Friday for their annual ladies' night, so if you're there, I can show you around," she offered. "If you have debt, then I can tell you who tips well and who doesn't. Plus, since you're new, I can also tell you who to stay away from and who is actually decent to their dates."

My throat was dry, but I managed to say, "Thank you."

"Well, it was nice to officially meet you," she replied happily. "However, I need to get back to my shopping."

"Yeah, so do I."

I watched as she wrapped her hands around her cart, then jetted off, leaving me to stand in a puddle of shame that I was never going to get free from. Maksim had taken me in front of an audience without letting me know, and what kind of monster did that? How many other people were going to randomly walk up to me, so that they can inform me that they'd seen me getting fucked by Maksim Barychev? He had ordered me to show him what kind of whore I could be, but that'd been for the audience, not him. When this was all said and done, I really was going to become a bratva whore, and I'd have no choice if I wanted to keep my grandfather at home with me.

I placed a hand on my stomach, doing my best not to throw up in the middle of the grocery aisle. I'd never felt so violated in all my life, and it felt like my skin was trying to crawl off my body with shame. Strangers had seen me at my most vulnerable, and they were bidding on me like I was an object to be used and played with, and why wouldn't they think that?

I finished my shopping on autopilot, then went straight home to hide from the world.

# CHAPTER 25

*Maksim ~*

Something was wrong with Katja, but I didn't know what. Granted, the woman was under a lot of stress, but this was something more. Though I had agreed to give her some space after the other night, it was beginning to feel as if she was purposely avoiding me, and the part of me that didn't trust easily wondered if she had changed her mind. It also had me wondering if she'd been playing me this entire time. What if her decision to 'double-cross' Nikel had been the plan all along?

At any rate, after passing me over in favor of work for the third time, I had ordered her to accompany me to Erato's, not giving her much of a choice. While I understood her not wanting her grandfather getting suspicious of her all-nighters, he would understand her going out with her friends on a Friday night, so she'd had no excuse when I had extended the request. In fact, the only reason that I hadn't pushed it before tonight was because Artur had assured me that she really was working, often working late nights from home. Apparently, Katja was good at her job and was often sought after.

Nevertheless, unlike the other times, instead of sending a car for her, I'd had Jurik drive me to her house, so that I could collect her myself. The plan was to speak with her grandfather soon, so it was time to quit treating her as if she were an option. Things had changed between us, and as soon as Morocco got back to us with whatever he could find, I was putting a guard on Katja, then we could begin making plans for a small ceremony since her grandfather was unable to get around easily.

So, after collecting her, I'd had Jurik drive us to Erato's, hoping that the crowd would tempt Nikel to come out, believing that he wouldn't be seen. Once a year, Erato's had a ladies' night, and it was basically a buffet for anyone looking to get lucky. With Nikel believing that Katja was a bratva whore, I was really hoping that he'd be stupid enough to come out. Most members of the bratva knew what he looked like, so we had eyes everywhere tonight, though nothing was guaranteed. Truthfully, I regretted not contacting the Sartoris before now, and that was all Katja's doing. Had she never come into the picture, we'd still be trying to figure this shit out on our own.

Regardless of whatever may or may not happen tonight, it was apparent that something was going on with Katja, and I was tired of waiting for her to tell me willingly. From the second that she had opened her front door to me, she hadn't uttered a single word, and now she was sitting next to me, silent as a tomb, answering my questions with only a nod or shake of her head. She had even declined a drink, not even asking for water. She was simply sitting next to me in the VIP booth, staring at her purse like it had the answers to all of life's mysteries.

"What is troubling you, Katja?" I finally asked. We were alone in the booth, so it wasn't a problem to speak freely.

"The same thing that's been troubling me for weeks," she lied.

"Look at me when I am speaking to you," I ordered.

When she slid her bright-colored eyes my way, I almost regretted asking her to do so. She was looking at me like I was a stranger, and I didn't like it. It was nothing like when she let me inside her, and I was surprised by how quickly her distance was pissing me off.

"Now, I will only ask once more," I warned her. "What is troubling you?"

"Usually, my grandfather is resting when you summon me," she said, and whatever she was about to say, I hoped that she wasn't lying, something that could easily be proven or disproven by one phone call to Artur. "He and Artur were in the kitchen tonight when I walked out of my bedroom, and when he saw the way that I was dressed, he grew suspicious."

"What did you tell him?" I asked, already knowing that I was going to call Artur.

Her jaw ticked before saying, "Well, since I very well couldn't tell him that Maksim Barychev was picking me up because I agreed to be his whore, so that he wouldn't kill me for betraying him with a man that was clearly out of his mind, I told him that I had a date with a guy that I met during my last field call." Though she probably wasn't lying because she knew that the truth was only one phone call away, there was still something off about her story. "He wished me a good evening, and I guess I'm just tired of lying to the only person in the world that loves me."

It was on the tip of my tongue to tell her that her grandfather wasn't the only person in the world that loved her, but even I knew that it was too soon to tell her something like that. Even if it was true, there was no way that she'd believe me, and why should she? This entire situation was a fucking mess, and we were no better. Luckily for me, Morocco Carrisi was good at his job, so I knew that we'd have something in a day or two.

"If you would like, we can leave," I said, offering a bit of an olive branch.

"Why?" she asked, her jaw still ticking. "Aren't we here for the same reason that we go anywhere? Aren't we here for Klive? Aren't we here to draw him out?"

"There will be other opportunities to draw him out," I replied evenly, confident that Nikel's patience was running low.

Her amber-colored eyes flashed with annoyance. "And have all this be for nothing? Every second that he roams free, my grandfather isn't safe-"

I grabbed her by the chin, squeezing it in between my fingers. "That will be the last time when you will suggest that I cannot keep your grandfather safe, Katja," I told her. "Artur is one of our best, and Nikel would have to kill him first to get to your grandfather."

"You say that like it's not possible," she fired back. "All it takes is one bullet that no one sees coming, and since it appears that Klive is always one step ahead of you guys, there's no real guarantee that Artur can keep my grandfather safe."

Her truth stung, and the man in me was having a very difficult time taking the hit without burning the entire city to the ground. Nothing was more crippling to a man than his woman telling him that she didn't feel safe with him, and that's essentially what Katja was telling me as she worried about her grandfather. She didn't trust me to protect her or her family, and that knowledge was emasculating as fucking hell.

I stared into her troubled eyes as I said, "No harm will come to your grandfather on my watch, Katja. I give you my word on that."

"How about you save your energy for finding Klive, instead of spouting off promises that you can't possibly keep," she spat, and the venom in her voice was real.

I squeezed her chin tighter in between my fingers. "What happened?" I hissed. "And do not tell me that the vitriol dripping from your voice is because of your concern for your grandfather. I will tolerate a lot from you, Katja. However, lying isn't one of those things."

Instead of answering me, she arched a brow as she asked, "Do you really think that it's wise for people to see Maksim Barychev arguing with his whore?"

*I wanted to strangle her.*

"Besides, the last thing that I need is for Klive to think that I'm ruining things between us," she went on. "If he really is watching, I'm supposed to be playing the part of meek arm candy to gain your trust, remember?"

While I was furious and wanted to argue her point, she wasn't wrong. The plan was for me to be falling under her spell enough to become vulnerable, not to engage in public fights, something that everyone knows that I'd never engage in when it came to an easy piece of ass.

I let go of her chin, then casually leaned back in the booth. "This conversation isn't over," I told her. "We will continue this discussion once we get home."

"I don't understand," she said. "What difference does my mood make? As long as I'm here, doing my part, who gives a shit about how I'm feeling?'

"Watch yourself, Katja," I warned. "I've already spoken to you about how you will address me."

Fire flashed in her eyes, and I had no doubt that she'd shoot me dead if she were quick enough to get her hands on any one of my guns. Now, I wasn't sure if that fire had always been there or if it was a result of having lived on her own for so long, but there was no doubt that Katja Volkov did not appreciate a man correcting her, and that was something that we were going to have to work on if we didn't want to end up killing one another.

At any rate, before she could say anything, Karik was approaching our table. *"Bratok,* I need a moment."

Not sure if this had to do with bratva business or Mindy and her family, I looked over at Katja, then said, "I'll be only a moment. Do not leave this table."

"What if I need the restroom?" she asked flippantly.

"Then you fucking hold it," I hissed, not caring that Karik could hear our exchange. "Do not leave this goddamn table, Katja. Do you hear me?"

"Perfectly," she bit out.

Praying that she wasn't going to make me kill her in a room fool of people, I stood up from the table, then followed Karik to find a private corner, though that was kind of hard to do in this crowd. Still, people knew better than to bother any members of the bratva.

# CHAPTER 26

*Katja ~*

It was said that we never knew what we were capable of until we had to do it, and I was finding myself in that exact situation now. When my grandfather had asked me about my night, shame had almost eaten me alive. However, instead of telling him that Maksim Barychev was going to parade me around town as the newest Kotov whore, I had lied to his face, making him believe that I was actually going out on a date with some nice, unassuming, irrelevant gentleman.

Things had only gotten worse when I had opened my front door to Maksim standing on the other side, deviating from our regular routine. While I'd known that I hadn't had a choice when he had summoned me to join him tonight, I still hadn't had enough time to wrap my mind around what I'd learned at the supermarket, and I honestly didn't know if I was hurt, angry, ashamed, or just empty inside.

I'd also be lying if I'd said that I hadn't thought about the bids coming in to be with me. While I never imagined that I'd ever be in this position, knowing that men were willing to pay up to twenty-thousand dollars to sleep with me made me understand a little more why women sold their bodies. It really was the easiest way to make money, and with that kind of income, my grandfather would want for nothing. If I kept my regular job, then I'd only need to have a few clients a month to keep my grandfather with me. While I had no idea if the bratva permitted a part-time arrangement, maybe I could do that and not want to kill myself so much afterwards.

It was also hard not to keep my eyes glued onto my purse like a lifeline. I had no idea how many men or women in this place had seen my body and knew what I looked like while having sex, and I almost couldn't breathe with the weight of humiliation that I felt. It was one thing to sell your body and do it in the privacy of a hotel room or wherever, it was quite another to be used on stage for complete strangers. Consent was also a key difference. Now, even though it wasn't my thing, I'd already proven that I'd do anything for my grandfather, so it wouldn't have been a big deal for Maksim to tell me what his plans had been. So, I just couldn't understand why he'd hadn't.

"Oh, I'm so glad you made it." I looked up from my purse to see Janet smiling down at me. "Is it okay if I sit?"

Since I didn't know the rules, I should have told her no, but I needed a friend in this world, and if I was going to be pimped out after all this, then I needed someone that could help me navigate through everything that I didn't know. Of course, that didn't mean that I was going to just give in if that was the plan. I could always take on a few guys until I made enough money to put me and my grandfather on a plane to another country. Again, I'd do anything for my grandfather.

"Yea, of course," I said, doing my best not to look or act damaged.

"So, I see that you're here with Maksim, but there are a lot of guys here tonight that you probably should get to know," she prattled on, sounding like she genuinely wanted to help me. "Now, there's a rumor that you're no longer available, but I think that's only until Maksim gets tired of you, so you really should know what your other choices are."

*'Until Maksim gets tired of you.'*

"No, yeah…you're right," I said, smiling at her. "I…I really appreciate you doing this for me."

"No problem" she replied sweetly. "Us girls have to stick together, right?"

I nodded. "Right."

"So, David Winston pays decent enough, but he's not a regular, so you can't depend on him as part of your steady income," she said as she pointed to a blonde man that had a sultry brunette on his lap. "Plus, if your hope is to mix a little pleasure with business, then he's not your man. He has no idea where a woman's clit is, but he's safe."

"Safe?"

Janet looked at me. "Yeah, he's not into rough sex or anything like that. He's missionary for the most part."

Needing to know, I asked, "What happens if a man gets *too* rough?"

"Luckily for most of us, there are a few girls that are into that," she answered. "If a man is looking to really knock a girl around during sex, then they're steered towards the girls that are willing to do that."

"Seriously?"

Janet nodded, "Never underestimate the power of money, and never underestimate what someone is willing to do for it when they've no choice. While those girls might have to suffer a knock to the head, a broken nose, or whip marks on their backs, they're also rich for their troubles."

My stomach clenched hard enough that I was grateful that I hadn't eaten anything before coming out tonight. Once upon a time, I would have said that I'd never be one of those women that would allow a man to beat me for money, but once upon a time, I also would have said that I'd never whore myself out for anything in the world, yet here I was, doing exactly that, and the reason didn't matter. Everyone's reasons were noble to them, and since we all led different lives, it wasn't fair to say that my reason was more acceptable than someone else's.

"Oh, there's Jack Garrett," she said, pointing to a very tall man making his way up to the bar. "He's good in bed, and he also tips. With the prices that a lot of men pay to be with us, many don't tip, figuring that they're paying enough, but Jack tips on top of what he pays."

"That's...that's rather generous," I muttered for lack of something better to say.

Janet just nodded absently. "Even though he's not here tonight, Ben Hillar is also a good tipper, but he's an anal freak and likes it rough. Though he's not what I would call aggressive, he likes to plow his girls hard, and it's not always pleasant unless that's your niche."

"My niche?"

"Yeah...like, you know...there are some girls that have been conditioned to take two cocks up their ass, so I can't see a hard screw in the ass really hurting them much." Janet shrugged like this conversation wasn't absolutely horrific. "But just like we have some girls that are game for some violence, we also have girls that are down for multiple-partner situations. You'd be amazed at how many men get off on gangbangs. There's just something about watching a woman getting used that does it for these guys. Like they get off on reminding us of our place or something."

I didn't know what to say to that because I enjoyed rough sex, so was I advocating for that kind of behavior, or was I supposed to insist on respect in the bedroom to remind men that I was more than just three holes to be used as they saw fit? Even knowing what I knew now, I couldn't deny that Maksim Barychev was the best sex that I'd ever had, and that was partly due to the fact that he was rough and dominant in the bedroom.

*Christ, I was so confused.*

"Oh, there's Fredrick Milkov," she said, but her voice lowered to a whisper, almost like she wasn't supposed to speak his name out loud or something. "Stay away from him."

I glanced over at the man that she was looking at, and had it not been for being here and the tone of her voice, I would think that he seemed decent enough. He was dressed in a suit, his dark hair was styled expertly, and he looked like he belonged at the head of the table inside any boardroom across the country.

"Why?" I asked, merely curious.

"He's violent," she answered. "He likes to watch women being abused, and the more that she cries, the more he enjoys it. He's a sick puppy, and though the money is supposed to be worth it, I'm not sure if I agree with that. One girl was out of commission for two weeks because of him, but since she had agreed to it all, the bratva had let him be."

Just then, a pair of shocking blue eyes looked my way, and Fredrick Milkov was staring at me like he was already undressing me in his mind. His stare was intense and powerful enough to steal my breath, even from across the room. The vibe that I was getting off him had me believing every word that Janet had just said, and hopelessness already rose up to strangle me.

*What was I doing?*

"Am I interrupting?"

I looked up to see Maksim staring down at me and Janet, and it didn't take a rocket scientist to see that he was pissed. Granted, I never should have allowed Janet to get comfortable in our VIP booth, but I was driving blind here, so I was bound to make some bad decisions along the way.

"Oh, sorry," Janet quickly rushed out as she stood up. "We were just having a little...little girl talk."

"Well, you are done with your girl talk, *kukla,*" he told her.

"Of course," she muttered before quickly scurrying away.

As soon as Maksim was sitting next to me again, I asked, "What does *kukla* mean?"

"It means doll," he answered. "It's what I call all women that are empty-headed."

"She's not empty-headed," I snapped, automatically defending my only friend in the building.

Maksim's dark gaze narrowed at me. "She approached you without my permission, so that tells me that she is."

Seriously, what a fucking asshole.

# CHAPTER 27

*Maksim ~*

"Without your permission?" she echoed, clearly pissed.

"I am familiar with who Janet Woo is, Katja," I informed her. "She knows better than to approach my table without permission."

"Oh, I'll just bet you're familiar with her," she scoffed, and it was clear that we were going to give Nikel an unfavorable show whether it was a good idea or not.

"If that's your way of asking me if I've ever taken her up on her services, I have not," I clarified.

Despite that reassurance, Katja's buttery-colored eyes were still shooting flames my way. "Well, she was just trying to help me."

That caught me by surprise. "And in what way would she be able to help you?"

"She was telling me which men were the best tippers and-"

I had my hand wrapped around her neck before she could finish her sentence. "And why would you be needing to know which men in here are the best tippers?" I snarled at her. "And I must warn you that your answer may very well cost you your life, *lyublyu.*"

Instead of fear leaping into her eyes, the anger in them just blazed brighter. "Because isn't that the plan?" she spat, not even trying to remove my hand, not caring about our audience. "Aren't you planning on making me pay off my grandfather's care by becoming a bratva whore after you finally catch Klive? Isn't that why you fucked me in a room with an entire audience on the other side? That wasn't an audition to become *your* whore because we already knew that I didn't have a choice in that. You fucked me in that room to start the bids rolling for when you were finally done with me." Her eyes started to shine, but I knew enough to know that whatever tears were in her eyes, they were from rage and nothing more. "Well, Janet was just given me a short training course on who can help me pay for my grandfather's care the best."

107

I let go of her neck, but not because I wasn't furious, I let go because I was on the verge of losing her, and I knew it. "How did you find out about the room?"

"Are you fucking serious?" she hissed, not caring about my earlier warning. "That's what you have to say to me? That's what you're more concerned about?"

"Katja-"

"What kind of a monster does something like that to a woman?" she spat, and that's when I realized that she was also hurt on top of being livid. "While I was worried about Klive taking something that wasn't his to take, you were busy giving every private piece of me to complete strangers." The embattled tears finally cascaded down her face. "Not only did you take something from me, but you gave it away like a sale at the mall, and now I'm stuck walking around Port Townsend, wondering how many men on the street know what I sound and look like when I'm...when I'm..." Katja hurriedly reached up to wipe away her tears before letting out a calming breath. "Janet was just trying to help me be the best whore that the bratva needs me to be."

"I already told you that you belong to me," I reminded her. "I made that clear the other night."

"Yeah, and it's clear how you treat the things that belong to you," she shot back. "However, it doesn't really matter, does it? Whether I'm spreading my legs for you, your customers, or even Klive Simpson, I've shown my weakness, and I've made it clear that I'll do anything for my grandfather. So, what in the hell do I have to be mad about anyway, right?"

Though she was rightfully upset, I was still very aware of our audience. "We will discuss this later," I told her. "Right now, we need to do what we came here for."

"To show Klive that I've got you wrapped around my finger," she sneered. "Well, if he's watching, I guess it's time to put on another show."

Before I could ask her what she was talking about, Katja reached for my belt as she went to slide underneath the table, and I saw fucking red. Granted, I was at fault here, but she wasn't even giving me a chance to explain before making this worse than it already was.

I grabbed her by her arm to stop her from getting on her knees, then dumped her on my lap. As calmly as I could, I said, "If you ever behave like a whore in public again, I will kill you with my bare hands, Katja. That is not what you are here for, no matter how this all began. So, if I were you, I would take a step back to remember just who in the hell you are dealing with."

Refusing to relent, she said, "I know *exactly* who I'm dealing with. I'm dealing with a man that has absolutely no honor when it comes to women."

Livid beyond reason that she would dare question my honor, I was done with her. So, grabbing her by the arm, I stood up, forcing her to stand with me, and she barely had time to grab her purse before I was dragging her behind me to find one of the rooms that Erato's rented out to certain patrons.

Knowing that Jurik would handle anything that I needed, I didn't bother checking with management for a room. I simply checked each doorknob until I found one that opened.

As soon as I found one, I flung Katja inside, then locked the door behind me. I was so fucking incensed that it was a miracle that I could even speak. She was the first person to ever call my honor into question and live afterwards, and she was going to learn to never do it again.

"If you want to accuse me of not being honorable where women are concerned, then I'll show you exactly what it feels like to be a *real* bratva whore," I snapped.

Instead of retreating in fear, it looked like Katja was going to dig her heels in, and I wasn't sure whether that made me angrier or if I felt proud of her. The life that I led wasn't for the weak, and though Katja had started out as malleable, she was proving to be quite the opposite. She really was just enduring all of this for the sake of her grandfather, and that pleased me, though it wasn't anything that I was going to tell her right now. Right now, I had a point to prove, and she needed to learn her place. Yeah, it might be by my side, but she needed to learn that a queen still answered to her king, no matter what.

"Is that supposed to scare me?" she sneered, anger lacing every word out of her pretty mouth. "I've already had two different men threaten to kill me or rape me all within a couple of weeks, so you think that threatening to beat me is going to make me flinch? I tell you what, as much as I love my grandfather and would obviously do anything for him, at this point, a bullet to the head sounds a lot more agreeable than wondering if a man on the street is smiling at me because he's just being friendly or because he knows what my tits and pussy look like."

"Katja-"

"At the very least, Klive was honest about what he wanted," she went on. "You? You violated me in a way that beating me or raping me doesn't hold a candle to. Unless it's done in public, a beating or rape can be dealt with privately, minimizing the shame. What you did...you might as well have just recorded it, then put it on the internet. That's how violated I feel, Maksim. That's what you did to me."

"And your answer is to fuck other men?" I spat, the enormity of my error a glaring one. "Is that what you want? To be a bratva whore?"

"That's what you made me the second that you fucked me in that room!" she yelled.

"I made a mistake!" I yelled back, finally admitting it. "But I can fix it!"

"Go fuck yourself," she seethed, telling me exactly what she felt about my admission.

Avgust's words about losing her were coming back to haunt me, and for the first time in my adulthood, I felt the fear of losing something that mattered to me but also couldn't control. Unlike my brother, Katja hadn't chosen this life, so she wasn't committed to me in a way that Akim was. Plus, even if Akim had taken a different path, our blood bonded us in a way that we'd never be free from one another. Katja was standing in this room for her grandfather and nothing more.

I stepped to her, and though her body trembled slightly, she wasn't backing down. I reached up, then wrapped my hand around the back of her neck, holding her still. "I want you to listen to me, and I want you to listen well, Katja," I told her. "Whatever mistakes that I have made with you, they change nothing. You are mine, and the last thing that you will ever be is a whore for the bratva."

"Well, since you're a high-ranking member of the bratva, it seems as if I already am, Maksim," she fired back. "It's what I've *always* been since the beginning of all this."

"Then if that is all that you are content to be, then so be it," I hissed down at her, no longer giving a fuck about Nikel or giving Morocco time to find him. After tonight, we were no longer going to play Nikel's game. As much as I wanted to find the sonofabitch, I wanted Katja more. "So, now get on your knees and show me what a good whore you're going to be for me."

Defiant and looking so fucking stunning, she said, "Since you obviously can't be trusted with the pieces of myself that I've already given you, if you want me, then you're going to have to force me."

"You are overestimating my character, Katja," I told her. "That's a dangerous thing to do."

"You don't deserve me," she whispered both angrily and brokenly.

"I know, baby," I replied honestly. "I do know that."

Instead of slapping me or yelling some more, she surprised me by lowering herself onto her knees. However, when I remembered why she would do such a thing after what she'd found out, I realized that this woman was a lot stronger than I had originally given her credit for.

# CHAPTER 28

*Katja ~*

As I reached for Maksim's belt, I'd never felt so weak in all my life. Though I'd been screaming a good game, he and I both knew that I was always going to cave when it came to my grandfather. When it was all said and done, when push came to shove, when my feet were actually held to the fire, I was going to do whatever I could to save my grandfather from ever having his heart broken again. I was not going to be the one to put that look of loss on his face ever again.

With Maksim's hand lost in my hair, I freed him, then wrapped my lips around his cock, wishing that he didn't affect me the way that he did. My humiliation and shame were real, and I really did feel violated from what he'd done to me, but it was too late for me. I already had feelings for him, and since there was no way out of this situation right now, I had no idea how to separate those feelings from being with him. I was officially letting my feelings for him complicate something that really wasn't complicated. After what he'd done, I should hate him. Now that I knew what I knew, I should feel nothing for him but hate, but that's not how feelings worked. Feelings were often a chaotic mess, and they were also a lot stronger than logic at times. It was the reason that we stayed when we knew that we should leave; because when things felt good, they *really* felt good.

"Christ," Maksim hissed as his fingers fisted in my hair. "I definitely don't deserve how good you're making me feel, baby."

I wanted to ignore him and just martyr myself, but I wasn't that unfeeling. I wanted to be, and I wished like hell that I could be, but I wasn't. Everything about this situation was fucking me in a million different ways, but I couldn't deny that Maksim's voice always managed to send a shiver of dark need down my spine, and the woman in me liked being down here, and I hated myself for it.

However, as I took Maksim deep in the back of my throat, he didn't let me think on it for much longer. He pulled out of my mouth, and when I looked up at him, he immediately reached down, grabbed me by my shoulders, then hauled me to my feet.

Before I could ask him what he was doing, he turned me around, then pushed me onto the bed. "Get on all fours," he ordered.

I did as he'd commanded, and as soon as I was in position, I felt Maksim's hands on my left ankle, and my heart thumped at how he began removing my heels. It was such a seductive and intimate thing to do, and that's not what I wanted from him. I wanted to hate him for what he'd done to me, so the more that he pleasured me, the more I resented my weakness when it came to this man.

As soon as he removed my shoes, I felt him push my dress up over my hips, and because I'd chosen to wear light pink panties, I knew that he could see how wet I already was. I could say whatever I wanted, but my body betrayed me every time, and it was something that he wasn't above exploiting, and we both knew it.

I remained positioned as Maksim pulled my panties over my hips and down my thighs, and when he made no further move to actually take them off me, I knew that my little tirade hadn't made a difference to him, even if I'd been justified. He was going to fuck me like a whore not worth undressing, and he was going to prove his point while doing it.

The sounds of Maksim getting into position rang in my ears, and shame covered my face as I waited eagerly for what was coming next. My brain and body were not on the same page, and I feared that my body was always going to win that argument whenever it came to Maksim.

"See, baby," he said as I felt him run the head of his cock up and down my slit. "It'd be so easy to treat you like a whore, except for one thing." Maksim slid inside me with one purposeful thrust, making me cry out into the bedding. "I don't fuck whores without protection. In fact, you're the only woman that I have ever fucked without protection, so what do you think that makes you?"

Since I wanted to keep hating him, I didn't answer. I didn't want to feel significant. What Maksim had done was unforgiveable, so I needed to fuel my hate, and I couldn't do that if I let myself believe all his pretty words. It was bad enough that I wasn't strong enough to say no to him, so the last thing that I needed to do was let my feelings for him turn me into a complete fool.

When I felt a drop of spit hit my ass, pressure immediately pushed against the back of my eyes. He was going to do this here just to prove that he could, and I was going to let him because I was curious and eager enough not to care about the truth. I knew that it was going to hurt, but I also knew that it was going to feel phenomenal. Maksim wasn't a young man fumbling around in the dark, trying to find his way. No. He was a grown man that new exactly what he was doing and how to pleasure a woman.

Suddenly, Maksim grabbed a hold of my hair, then yanked me upward, my body arched uncomfortably. With his hips still pumping against my ass, his other hand slid between my legs, then started playing with my clit. He wasn't going to let me hide inside my head, and I should have expected as much.

"You're mine, Katja," he grunted in my ear. "Whatever was between us when we first met no longer exists." I let out a low whimper as his fingers manipulated my clit into a frenzy. "Your motives for approaching me no longer exist, and my desire to make you pay for that error no longer exists. What is between us now is the only thing that matters, but if you disagree with me, then I'll still be more than happy to treat you like a dirty slut. If you want me to treat you like a *kukla*, then I will."

With a cry stuck in my throat, I came all over Maksim's dick as his fingers showed me no mercy. My hands had to latch onto his forearm to help keep me upright, and the way that he rode me through my orgasm was making everything wrong about this situation disappear.

"Fuck, you're hot for it," he groaned right before pushing me back down on the bed by my neck. "You can say whatever the fuck you want to me, but we both know that your cunt is already addicted to my cock. We both know that you love playing the whore for me, and I'm going to prove it."

My fingers fisted in the bedding as Maksim pulled out of my pussy, then went immediately to working the head of his dick into my ass. I had to concentrate to control my breathing as a stinging pain shot up my spine, the sensation a foreign one. I'd never done this before, but it didn't take a genius to recognize that Maksim was probably not the man to break a woman in like this. He was simply too big to skip the preparations.

When he finally breached my opening, I let out a painful gasp, doing my best to calm down, knowing that if I told him to stop, then he would. However, that would feel too much like losing, and I wasn't quite ready to admit defeat.

"Fuck, your ass feels so fucking tight," he grunted as he kept sliding deeper inside me. "I'm not going to last with how tight you're squeezing me."

I felt another bead of spit hit my ass, and my body clenched with how dirty that felt. Using actual lubricants would feel more civilized than what he was doing now, but I supposed that's why we weren't using any. I had no doubt that this room contained a whole drawer full of condoms, lubricants, and whatever else was needed to have a good time."

"Maksim…" I finally choked out, surrendering.

"Shh, baby," he said behind me, his voice sending a shiver down my spine. "Let me take care of you."

Soon, Maksim was invading my body with smooth, even, deliberate strokes, and though it took a while, his deep thrusts started to feel good. The sting was still there, but it was being overshadowed by the decadent feeling of having a cock buried in my ass for the first time. Maksim's fingers were digging into my hips as he made me take every inch of him, and I could feel myself leaking down my thighs. There was just something about being given permission to be bad when we'd been told our whole lives that we'd better be good.

"Maksim..." I panted, already pushing my ass back for more. "Oh, God..."

"Take that dick like a good girl, *lyublyu,*" he grunted, his hips moving faster, his dick hitting my g-spot, even through my ass. "Show me how much you like my cock in your ass."

"Maksim...don't stop..." I cried out shamefully, my body giving itself over to him once again.

He yanked me back up by my hair. "Is my pretty little whore going to cum for me? Does getting fucked in the ass do it for you, baby?"

"Fuck you..." I choked out as I came from the brutal force of his thrusts, my body an already trembling mess.

"I'm never going to let you go," Maksim vowed, a dark laugh lacing his words. "I'm keeping you forever, Katja."

"I...I hate you..." I whimpered as pleasure weakened me everywhere. "I hate...you..."

Maksim let out a deep roar as he emptied his cock inside my ass, and all I could do was lay there while Maksim marked the only part of me that there'd been left to mark. I'd been officially claimed by him everywhere, and I no longer knew up from down. All I knew was that this was my life now, and things would be so much easier if the only thing that I felt for him was hate.

"This changes nothing," I finally said, lying through my teeth as my body collapsed on the bed.

"I know, baby," he replied quietly, though not caring in the least.

# CHAPTER 29

*Maksim ~*

After dropping Katja off at her home, I had immediately texted Avgust that I needed to speak with him, and because the man's sleep cycle was just as unhealthy as my own, he had replied for me to go ahead and stop by. Though I could have waited until the morning to speak with him, I hadn't wanted to. He was the only one that could approve my change of plans, and I hadn't wanted to put it off any longer. I'd lost any chance at Katja's love, and while I hadn't ever imagined that it could happen to me, it'd had.

As soon as Avgust answered the door, he asked, "Do we need drinks for this?"

I nodded. "Absolutely."

However, instead of going into his office, Avgust led me into his kitchen, and all that told me was that all his household staff was already gone for the night, and that all his guards were outside. If not, he would have taken this conversation to a more private room. Again, the man took no chances now that he had a family.

"So, what is troubling you, *bratok?*" he asked as he began opening cupboards.

I took a seat at the kitchen island before telling him why I was here. "You were right," I told him. "Katja found out about Millie's before I could tell her and explain our plan, and now she hates me."

Avgust didn't gloat or tell me those dreaded four little words. Instead, he just poured our drinks as he let my words play over in his head. I was lucky that Avgust hadn't ever kicked me when I'd been down, and I was thankful that he wasn't going to start now.

After sliding my drink across the counter, he finally asked, "What is it that you need from me?"

"I'm done with my plan to draw Nikel out," I informed him. "I want Katja with me, and I want her grandfather safe from any threats."

"If that's what you want, then she can no longer work starting now, Maksim," he pointed out. "Even if Nikel wasn't an issue, she'd have to change careers." Avgust shrugged as he added, "Or come work for us. It's no secret that we could use some technical support."

"What I have learned over the course of these past couple of weeks is that there isn't anything that she won't do for her grandfather," I replied easily. "Getting her to quit her job won't be a problem."

Avgust's hazel eyes regarded me carefully. "Maksim, while I understand that your intelligence level makes it hard for you to connect with us mere mortals at times, you would not be helping yourself if you *force* any more changes in Katja's life."

"Well, what is it that you suggest I do?" I retorted. "She already hates me, so I can't see asking her nicely working out for me."

"While your point is valid, you should probably do something to alleviate that hate, instead of feeding it," he advised. "And forcing her to quit her job will just feed it more."

"Look, as far as I'm concerned, I have the rest of our lives to work on her hate for me," I told him. "What I need right now is for her to be with me and for her grandfather to be safe. Once we get them both secured, then we can scour the streets for Nikel."

Just then, Avgust's phone chimed, and when he pulled it out of his pocket to look at it, his brows jumped in surprise. "It's Sartori."

"It's about fucking time," I hissed.

Avgust immediately answered the phone, then placed it on speaker. "This is Kotov," he answered.

"I've got Morocco with me," Nero announced, getting straight to the point. "Though it's late, I figured that you might not want to wait to hear what he's found out."

"You would be correct," Avgust replied smoothly. "I also have Maksim here with me, and this call is on speaker."

"I was able to tap into the cameras and find that Nikel Ovchinnikov is actually staying on Morongo Street, though there's no apartment in his name, nor have I been able to find out which apartment since none of the apartment complexes have cameras," Morocco said, getting straight to it. "The fact that each building is fifteen stories high and have ten apartments to each floor, it's like finding a needle in a haystack without anything in his name."

"Can you tell us which building, at least?" Avgust asked.

"It's the third one on the left of Morongo Street," he answered. "Though there's six buildings, that's the one that I keep seeing him go into after tracking him from when he leaves Maksim's girl. However, there are no cameras on the west end of the apartments."

"Meaning?" I asked.

"Meaning that he could easily be leaving out the backdoor to another one of the buildings, but we'd never know since there are no eyes on that side," he explained. "He could easily be hiding in plain sight, and since he's managed to remain undetected this long, he shouldn't be underestimated."

"What about any familiar faces around the clubs?" Avgust asked. "According to Katja, he's watching Akim and Maksim, and often knows where they are."

"I found a familiar face at all three locations that you gave me, and while I was able to pull up a clear enough picture, if it's Ovchinnikov, then the man is great at disguises," he said. "So, it's either him or he found someone else to work with him. However, I'm betting that it's him."

"Because why not use this new person to approach Katja, correct?" I surmised. "Why take the chance to be seen if he has someone else to take the risk?"

"Exactly," Morocco replied. "I also ran every name in the third apartment building, but nothing flagged. So, he's either shacking up with someone, or else he's squatting in an empty apartment."

"Are there many?" I asked. "Empty apartments, I mean."

"Only three," he answered. "So, you might want to check them first. I'll send over the numbers when I send over the pictures."

"Is there anything else?" Avgust asked.

"When he's stalking Maksim, he's driving a dark Chevy truck. However, when he's stalking Maksim's girl, he's on foot," he added. "I'm not sure if that's significant or not, but it still should be noted."

"Okay," Avgust said. "Thank you for the help, and you'll have your money as soon as we get everything."

Nero let out a low chuckle. "Forget the payment, Kotov. Mrs. Sartori sends her well wishes."

"I'd rather pay you," Avgust remarked dryly.

"As I completely understand that viewpoint, what my wife wants matters more to me than what you would prefer," Nero replied smoothly. "Of course, we can continue to argue about it if you wish."

"Okay, I have to ask," I blurted. "Why? Why does she do this for us?"

"She doesn't do it for us, gentlemen," Nero answered honestly. "She does it for the women. My wife is a firm believer that no man is truly deserving of the woman that loves him, so this is her way of helping *them* out. Never us."

"She's not wrong," Avgust grumbled.

"No, she's not," Nero easily agreed.

"Well, tell her that we appreciate the gesture," Avgust replied graciously. "Hopefully, this will be the last time that we'll require your services."

"You know, Maksim's girl is quite talented," Morocco stated. "If she can hone her skills a little bit better, then she can probably get you through some tight spots."

"How do you know that she's talented?" I asked, though I already knew the answer.

"The same way that I know everything about any name that you've ever handed me," he retorted.

"Fair enough," I chuckled.

"Goodbye, gentlemen," Nero said before ending the call.

After Avgust slipped his phone back in his pocket, he asked, "What do you want to do now?"

"Since the grandfather is more important to Katja than her own safety, I'm going to speak with Artur to let him know the change of plans," I told him. "My house is big enough for both Mr. Antonov and us to both have our privacy."

Avgust arched a brow. "While I recognize that you are used to doing whatever you want, my advice is to speak with Mr. Antonov yourself, Maksim. Though manipulative, if you can get into Mr. Antonov's good graces, then maybe it'll help with Katja's antagonism towards you."

"Fine," I relented, seeing the logic behind the suggestion. "I will speak with Mr. Antonov Monday morning, after Katja has left for work. I don't need her making our conversation more awkward than it will no doubt already be."

Avgust snorted. "You definitely have your hands full."

"I'll also call Akim to inform him of the change of plans," I added.

Avgust's brows furrowed. "I'm still curious why it seems as if he's after you more than Akim."

"Maybe he holds me more responsible since I'm the oldest," I suggested, shrugging.

"Okay, we can find that all out once we find him. For now, do what you need to do, Maksim."

"Thank you, Pakhan," I replied easily, ready to do just that.

# CHAPTER 30

*Katja ~*

Thankfully, I wasn't walking gingerly anymore, so I wasn't going to have to come up with a lie for why I was walking funny. All weekend long, I'd been able to convince my grandfather that my 'date' had taken me dancing, and being wholly out of shape, I'd woken up sore. Luckily for me, he had just laughed before encouraging me to get some more exercise.

At any rate, I also hadn't heard from Maksim all weekend, except for a few texts that came across like threats. If I hadn't already been sleeping with Maksim, they would have come across like something from a stalker's handbook. His texts had been to remind me that I was his, and to also remind me that I didn't have a choice in the matter.

*It'd been an exhausting weekend.*

That was probably why I hadn't been paying attention to my surroundings when I felt a strong arm wrap around my waist as soon as I got out of my car. The hand over my mouth silenced my surprised scream, and it took only a few seconds before I realized what this was, and of fucking course.

"If you scream or draw any unnecessary attention, I will gut you, *milaya devushka.*"

I gave Klive a quick nod to let him know that I'd heard him. However, as soon as he moved his hand from my mouth, I did ask, "What are you doing?"

"Finally taking matters into my own hands," he answered cryptically. "Now, we're going to walk over to my truck, and you're going to get in like a good captive. If not, I will leave you here, then drive straight over to your house, then kill your grandfather before the police can even get there."

Even though I knew that Artur was with him, I wasn't sure if I still trusted him completely. While you'd think that Artur would have the upper-hand, I couldn't risk my grandfather's life on that. Plus, wasn't this what we'd been hoping for? To finally bring Klive out into the open?

With my heart beating rapidly inside my chest, I followed Klive to his truck, deciding to wait this out. While it could be the worst decision of my life, I hadn't grown up with a kidnapping plan in place for situations like this one.

Once we got in his truck, I asked, "Why me, Klive? Why are you doing this?"

He ignored me.

He ignored me all the way until we passed an abandoned warehouse just outside the city limits, and I really was a goddamn fool. From day one, I'd been playing this all wrong because they didn't prepare you for this shit in school. Oh, they warned you of stranger-danger, but not of getting hijacked by the Mafia and whatever came with such an ordeal.

I also realized that I'd been living in a delusional state since the second that Klive had sat down at my lunch table. I had convinced myself that I could keep my grandfather safe when I'd never had the control to do that. I'd been nothing but a pawn between Maksim and Klive, and I'd been too naïve or arrogant to see it before. They'd been pulling my strings this entire time, and I'd been too stupid to realize it. I'd let my emotions and desperation cloud my common sense, and because of that, I'd gotten into Klive's truck without a struggle. I'd gotten into his truck, and now I was going to die for my stupidity, and quite frankly, I deserved it.

*Christ, how could I have been so stupid?*

When Klive finally parked his truck in the dead grass in back of a rotting house, I thought about making a run for it. After all, bullets were the only things that you couldn't outrun. Yeah, a knife might get me if he stabbed in the perfect place to kill me, but I still had a fighting chance against a knife.

However, all my grand plans quickly went up in smoke when he turned off the engine, saying, "I also have a gun, Katja. I just didn't want to pull it out in case you decided to fight me. I couldn't afford it accidentally going off and calling attention to what I was doing."

"Well, that was very thought out of you," I drawled out, suddenly feeling so damn exhausted.

To prove his point, Klive finally pulled out his gun, and without another word, we both got out of the truck as I started to think up a different plan. Now, in the movies, you're supposed to get the maniac talking and try to connect with him, but what was there to talk about? I already knew that he was here because of Maksim, so what more could I possibly learn that would help me? What would getting to know each other better get me? Yeah, conversation might stall him, but to what end?

When we finally entered the house, it looked like it might fall down around us at any moment, which might not be a bad thing in all honesty. I was also curious as to how he knew about this place, but Klive's resources were the least of my problems right now.

"What am I doing here?" I finally asked. "Why are you doing this?"

"Sit down," he ordered as he ushered me into the living room, a dusty couch right in the middle of the room, two wooden chairs near the front window.

"Where?"

Klive grabbed one of the chairs, then placed it in the center of the room. "Here."

I did as he'd ordered, and as soon as I sat down, he grabbed some rope that I just noticed had been laying across the couch. Resigned, I didn't fight as he tied me to the chair, praying that my wits would get me out of this since I was no match for him in strength, and definitely no match for the gun.

When Klive was done tying me to the chair, he said, "I saw you and Maksim arguing at Erato's the other night. Why were you fighting with him?"

"I bought him a drink, and he took exception," I answered, sticking to the truth as much as possible.

"You're lying!" he yelled right before backhanding me across the face, the force of the hit making my eyes water.

"I'm not lying," I semi-lied. "He felt insulted that I would pay for our outing."

"Why fight with him?" he asked. "You're supposed to be sucking his dick to get information for me. Why would you fight with him, knowing that he could easily cast you aside and ruin all our plans?"

"We weren't fighting," I lied again. "He got mad, but I wasn't fighting with him."

"You know, I picked you because there was no one else. Samara Kotov and Masha Andreev are too well guarded, and Akim is always with his family," he bit out. "With Maksim always being alone, he was the better target, and using a perfect stranger with everything to lose was the best plan."

Panic gripped my chest, but I did my best to keep it under control. "So, what's the plan now?"

"Everyone knows that indifference is the true definition of apathy," he said. "So, since Maksim cares enough about you to argue with you, the plan has changed."

I shook my head, my left eye still stinging a bit. "What are you talking about?"

"I'm going to make a trade," he announced. "Maksim for you."

I laughed.

Despite it all, I laughed.

Honestly, I couldn't help myself.

Looking into his dark eyes, I asked, "Do you really believe that Maksim Barychev is going to trade his life for some random pussy?" No matter what Maksim might have said to me in bed, there was no way that he was going to sacrifice himself for a woman that he'd only been fucking for a few weeks. "You're insane."

"Well, we'll see, won't we?" he replied coldly. "Shall we call him now?"

Thankfully, I'd had enough sense to erase all the texts between me and

Maksim. Granted, I had also erased all the texts and calls that I'd gotten from Klive, but that'd been in a futile attempt to pretend that my life was normal.

"You can call him, but I can guarantee you that Maksim won't care that you have me," I told him. "He might orchestrate an exchange to get to the bottom of this, but he's not going to care if you kill me, Klive. You're…you might as well just let me go. I'm not the bargaining chip that you think I am."

"Even if Maksim doesn't think you're worth the trade, that doesn't mean that I can't have some fun with you in the meantime," he remarked with a sneer, and I knew that I wasn't going to leave here alive.

I thought about my grandfather, and pain hit the center of my chest like a two-by-four. There was no telling how long it'd be before someone found my body out here, and I had no idea if he was going to be able to withstand me missing before finding out the truth. He was going to be left alone with so much violence left behind, and my heart was breaking for him

I watched as Klive dug into my purse to get my phone out, and he was going to have to kill me before I let him rape me. Maybe that was a stupid choice to make, but I wanted to leave this world a fighter. Albeit a stupid one, but a fighter, nonetheless. Even if my grandfather would never know, it'd be enough that I knew that I'd gone out fighting, hoping to make him proud.

When Klive finally walked over with my phone in his hand, he ordered me to unlock it, and when I did, he said, "For your sake, you better have made a better impression on him than you think."

"You're making a mistake, Klive," I said, hoping to make him listen. "It's not too late to still stick with our original plan."

"It became too late the second that you failed me, *milaya devushka.*"

# CHAPTER 31

*Maksim ~*

I stared at the empty room, hoping that it would work. I could always build a guest house to accommodate Mr. Antonov, but I knew that Katja would probably feel better if he was actually living with us inside the house. Though he was going to be guarded better than The Pope, it was about comfort and familiarity for Katja, and there was no denying how much her grandfather meant to her.

So, after speaking with Artur last night, I had arranged to have one of the guest rooms emptied, trusting that Katja could decorate it to suit her grandfather's preferences. The room was large enough for whatever he might need, and there was a restroom just one door over. Of course, if it would make things easier, I could always convert his room to add a small restroom, but Artur had assured me that the man wasn't invalid. He had simply needed assistance at times.

At any rate, with Katja at work, Artur aware of the changes, and Avgust giving me the green light to move forward with sweeping the apartments on Morongo, all I needed to do was speak with Mr. Antonov to discuss my intentions towards his granddaughter. Now, while I couldn't see him too pleased with the fact that his granddaughter was going to marry into the Russian Bratva, I also trusted that the man was smart enough to recognize that there wasn't anything that he could do about it.

As I looked over the room, my phone rang, and when I pulled it out of my pocket to see that it was Katja calling me, my back immediately straightened. Since she was supposed to be at work, she'd only be calling me if it was an emergency.

"Katja?"

"No, Barychev," came a male voice over the line. "It's not Katja."

My blood turned cold in my veins, already knowing who it was on the other end. "Nikel."

"Ah, so my secret is out," he taunted. "I am curious to know why you would automatically connect me with the lovely Katja."

"No one else in this city would dare go near her if they knew that I was entertaining her," I replied smoothly, doing my best not to give us both away. If he found out that she double-crossed him, he'd kill her before I could find her. "They also would not be stupid enough to call me about it."

"That is a fair point," he conceded. "But that still doesn't tell me how you know my real name."

"We are Russian Bratva, so we already knew who you were," I pointed out coolly. "Plus, did you honestly believe that we would not do everything necessary to find out who was behind Samara Kotov's kidnapping? Did you already forget the lovely little chat that you had with Avgust that night?"

"Yes, the lovely Samara," he drawled out humorously, ignoring the reminder about Avgust. "You know, I wanted to go after her again, but Kotov sure does have her guarded nicely. Then I thought about going after her sister, but she is also well guarded."

"What are you doing with Katja?" I asked, hoping that my question sounded casual enough.

"Well, at first, I was going to trade her life for yours," he replied easily. "I know enough that you would never give up Akim, so the plan was to go after him once I was done with you. However, Katja has informed me that you would never trade your life for a random whore, so I have decided to have some fun with her until she is no longer of any use to me. After all, whether you hold any affection for her or not, I am curious to taste what made you keep her around for so long."

My hand gripped my phone so hard that it was a miracle that it wasn't shattering in my ear. If I offered to trade my life for Katja, then he'd know how important she was to me, and that would just give him more leverage. However, if I did nothing, then he was going to keep her and rape her until he was done with her, and I couldn't allow that, either.

"Then why call me?" I challenged. "If you've changed your plan to get to me, then why call?"

"For the same reason that Louie took Samara," he replied. "To show you just how close I am, and to prove that I can get to you first."

"Then why haven't you come for me?" I bit out. "Why are you using women as your pawns? Why do you not come for me like a fucking man, Nikel? Is it because you are not? Is it because you know that you are outmatched against the bratva? Or is it because you are weak and know that you are nothing in comparison to me and Akim?"

As I insulted him, I quickly raced to my office to grab a burner cell. I needed to move fast if I had any chance of saving Katja. So, once I pulled out an extra phone from my desk, I fired off a text to Avgust, asking him to call Sartori and get Morocco to trace Katja's number. While I wasn't underestimating Nikel's intelligence, I was also willing to try anything to find

Katja right now.

"If that is the case, then why have you not caught me by now, Barychev?" he asked, purposely rubbing salt in that particular wound. "It has been five years since I have come here."

"Because you were not a priority for us," I semi-lied. "At first, we thought you were just riffraff, nothing important. Just someone that was irritating the syndicates."

"But surely the kidnapping of Samara Kotov changed all that, no?" he retorted. "Yet, an entire year later, you still have not found me. Yet, I am supposed to believe that you are smarter than I am?"

"It is hard for me to credit any man that would use women for his vendetta," I informed him as the burner chimed in my other hand.

Unknown: *Done. As long as her phone stays on, he should b able 2 find her*

Ignoring that, he said, "You know, I really thought that Katja would be the one to help me with my plan. She is very beautiful, and I certainly do not have to tell you what an incredible body she has." Though very true, I knew that he was just trying to get a reaction out of me. "It is the eyes. I was certain that you would be powerless against them. I was certain that you would fall under her spell when she was on her knees before you, your cock in her mouth, those eyes of hers looking up at you for approval."

"Do you take me for a fool, Nikel?" I asked, pacing my office. "Even if I did agree to trade my life for Katja's, we both know that you would kill her the first chance that you got. Witnesses are never good in situations like these."

"True," he agreed. "However, Katja can be controlled by her love for her grandfather, and so all I would have to do is keep from killing him, and that would ensure that she remained my loyal whore."

With no sense in arguing the truth, I said, "You still have not told me what this is all about, Nikel. While I know who you are and why you are here, what are you waiting for? Why have you not just picked me off already. While Akim and I are rather vigilant and guarded well, you still could have killed us long ago. After all, you know what we look like while you have been in disguise this entire time."

"Because I am not in this as a suicide mission," he spat, his emotions finally getting the better of him. "While I want you and your brother to pay for our father's sins, my plan for revenge does not include martyring myself."

Just then, the burner phone chimed again, a different number this time.

Unknown: *Give him a reason 2 expect a call from u b4 u hang up. It's easier if the phone stays on*

My guess was that the text was from Sartori or Morocco, but it hardly mattered. Right now, I would take any help that I could.

"So, what is the plan?" I asked, my mind racing. "You have called me, we have chatted, and we are still no closer to taking care of this situation. So, what is it that you want from me, Nikel?"

"If you will not trade your life for Katja, then trade it for Akim," he replied. "If not Akim, then your sister-in-law or their children. After all, it would be nothing to pick them off."

That's when the truth finally dawned on me, and it was clear that Nikel was a bad shot. He kept making references to not wanting to martyr himself for his revenge, but he'd only by martyring himself if we caught him, and the only way that we'd catch him was if he was close enough to catch. If he was a bad shot, then he'd have to be close enough to get the job done correctly, and he knew that there'd be no escaping the bratva like that.

"Deal," I replied, letting him believe that he'd won. "But if I am going to give my life for the greater good, then you need to let Katja go."

There was a moment of silence on his end, and that's when I knew that I'd fucked up. "Well, I guess I was correct after all."

"Nikel-"

"Keep your phone on you, Barychev," he chuckled darkly. "I'd hate for you to miss an important call."

With that, he hung up, making me grab the first thing that I reached for, then throwing the decanter of whiskey across the room.

Nikel was going to kill her.

He was going to kill her, and it was all my fault.

# CHAPTER 32

*Katja ~*

My phone kept going off, and like an asshole, Klive kept checking it, making taunts about how I must be late for work, which would bring on a whole other host of problems if my supervisor or one of my co-workers decided to call the police for a welfare check.

The asshole also hadn't shared the conversation that he'd had with Maksim with me. While I'd heard bits and pieces at the start of it, Klive had ended up walking into the kitchen for the rest of their talk, so I had no idea what the hell was happening, and I just didn't have the energy to ask. I needed to find a way out of here, and as long as I was tied to this goddamn chair, my options were limited. In hindsight, I should have taken off running when I'd had the chance. In fact, knowing what I knew now, I should have just called the police when Klive had first approached me. Instead, I'd chosen to turn my life into a bad Lifetime movie, and I hadn't helped the situation by continuously making wrong choices.

*I really was fucking stupid.*

"You know, it is quite addicting when you finally have all the power," Klive remarked as he walked back into the living room from the bathroom. Though there wasn't any running water here, I still appreciated that he hadn't whipped his dick out in front of me to piss on the floor. "It is always a woman that is a man's downfall, no?"

"I don't know what you're talking about," I said as I watched him set my phone on one of the dirty windowsills.

Klive looked back at me, his brown eyes so much like Maksim's. "You said that you did not matter to Barychev," he replied quietly. "You said that you were just a random whore."

"I am," I insisted, dread beginning to creep down my spine.

"Then why is he willing to trade his life for both his brother *and* you?" he asked, surprising me.

I started shaking my head. "You're wrong. Maksim would never sacrifice himself for me."

"Well, I hate to break it to you, but that is exactly what he did."

"No, you're wrong. You…you must have…have misheard, or…or they're setting you up." I shook my head again. "I'm irrelevant to that man. Trust me."

"Then let us test that theory, shall we?" he smirked as he made his way over to me.

"What do you mean?" I asked, doing my best to keep my voice steady.

Klive walked over to stand behind me, and when I felt his hot breath on my ear, it was all that I could do not to scream. "I need you to smile into the camera, *milaya devushka.*"

"For what?" I bit out.

"For the show, of course," he chuckled darkly, and I almost threw up everywhere.

Klive wasted no time reaching over to begin unbuttoning my shirt, and had I known that I was going to be kidnapped and molested this morning, then I would have chosen to wear a regular work t-shirt with my jeans, instead of the button-up option that we had. Normally, I dressed casually if I was scheduled to stay in the office, but when I had scheduled maintenance visits, I wore our company's shirts.

When Klive was finished unbuttoning my shirt, he pulled the lapels apart, showing off my bra, and I couldn't help but think of that night at Millie's. Men kept showcasing my body without my permission, and the cold reality of helplessness was a bitter pill to swallow. Before all this, I used to think that I was strong, and like most women, had played out scenarios in my head of what I would do if I was ever attacked, but the reality was so much different than the false bravery in our heads. Sure, I could come up with all kinds of excuses of how I'd been manipulated, but I'd never been big on blaming the other guy for my poor choices, and not going to the police when Klive had first approached me had been the worst decision of my life, no matter how noble my reasons.

Nevertheless, I wasn't going to feed Klive's sick thrills. So, instead of smiling into the camera, I looked down at my lap as he used his knife to cut through the middle of my bra, exposing me. I needed to get out of here before he raped or killed me, and I needed to be smart about it.

When Klive's hand cupped my left breast, it was all that I could do not to start crying, raging, and falling apart. It was all that I could do to keep my wits about me and not just fucking lose it. It was hard not to just start despising the male species as a whole. The only thing saving me was that I knew for a fact that there were good men out there. My father had been one of them, and my grandfather was still the best person that I'd ever known.

"*Lisus Khristos*, you feel good, *milaya devushka,*" he said as he fondled me, his voice a disgusting blanket of evil. "No wonder Barychev is willing to die for you."

I didn't say anything to that because he was wrong, of course. Even if Maksim really did care for me, Avgust Kotov wasn't going to let him start a bloodbath for some piece of ass that he was screwing. As powerful as Maksim Barychev was, it was Avgust Kotov that ran things, and Klive kept forgetting that important fact.

His other hand came up to cup my other breast, and all I could think about was how he wasn't holding the knife any longer or the gun. Both of his hands were occupied, and that gave me hope. If he wanted to rape me enough to be careless, then I had a chance.

"I cannot wait to send him a video of my dick in your mouth," he whispered in my ear, and I almost laughed.

*That was my way out of this.*

As a plan started developing in my head, Klive kept molesting me, but hope was stronger than fear at this moment, and so I forced myself to concentrate on what to do next, rather than give in to the shame that was definitely going to hit me later. After all, my stupidity and compliance were what had placed me in this chair, and self-awareness really was an unforgiving bitch.

When he was finally done playing the part for the camera, he stopped touching me, then walked over to where he had placed the phone. After turning it off, I watched his fingers fly over the screen, and I knew that he was sending the video to Maksim, and if that wasn't irony working overtime, then I didn't know what was. Once upon a time, Maksim had been perfectly fine with taking me in front of an audience, but now that *he* was the actual audience, I couldn't help but wonder how he'd feel about that.

"It is only fair, do you not think?" Klive asked after he set the phone back on the windowsill.

"What is?" I asked, refusing to let him shame me.

"Our father used my mother as his whore, so it seems fitting that I use Maksim's woman for that same purpose," he answered, and it was incredible how much their family dynamics was none of my business. "I had to spend years watching our father come and go without any regard for anyone but himself, so it only seems right to make Maksim feel the same way since Akim is already married."

"I honestly have no idea what in the hell you're talking about," I told him.

Klive walked over to me, then sat down on the questionable wooden coffee table in front of me. His brown gaze regarded me intently as he asked, "Have you ever seen a desperate person fight for their life?"

"What?"

"As your life flashes before your eyes, you will desperately grab onto anything that you think might be able to save you," he went on as if I hadn't spoken. "You don't care what it is, either. Your panicked hands will reach out for anything that will spare you. You don't care how ridiculous or impossible it might seem. Even if your mind knows that it cannot save you, you still try. You try to save yourself with whatever is available, and you are what is available to me, *milaya devushka*. Since I cannot get to Akim or his family without it costing my own life, you are the next best thing. Even if I did believe that Maksim held no affection for you, I would still use you because you are the only thing within my reach right now."

"So…" I let out a hollow laugh. "So, you're doing all this to me because I'm *convenient?* Are you serious right now?"

"I did not come all this way from Russia, then bide my time for five years to fail," he said, still acting like I knew what he was talking about. "Though intentional or not, the Sartoris and O'Briens have helped thwart my plans over the years, and I am done waiting."

"I don't get it," I bit out, desperation threatening to make an appearance. "Why not just shoot Maksim or Akim dead?"

"I do not want to martyr myself for my revenge," he stated simply.

I shook my head in disbelief. "That's the part that I think you don't understand. The second that you decided to go up against the Kotovs, you were already a dead man. It doesn't matter if you kill me or not, Klive. As long as you're alive and a threat to Maksim or Akim, they won't stop until you're dead. How can you not see that?"

"They would have to follow me to Russia to accomplish that," he replied coolly.

"Because you think that they won't?" I countered. "Maksim Barychev is the second-highest ranking member of the Russian Bratva, and if you think that they won't follow you into the bowels of Hell to find you, then you're very mistaken."

"Well, we will see about that, will we not?" he huffed with misplaced attitude.

"*We* won't," I retorted. "But *you* definitely will."

# CHAPTER 33

*Maksim ~*

Avgust was staring at me as I paced my office, waiting for Nero or Morocco to call us back or send a text with Katja's whereabouts, and he was wise enough not to give me any half-ass platitudes about how everything was going to be okay or how she was going to be fine. After what had happened to his wife, he knew well enough that things weren't always fine.

There was also the fact that someone was going to have to tell her grandfather what happened if the worst came to be. That was not how I wanted to meet Mr. Antonov for the first time, but I wouldn't let anyone else tell him. This was my error, and my penance would be looking that man in his eyes and telling him that his granddaughter had been hurt because of me. It also didn't matter that Nikel had chosen her all on his own. The second that I started feeling something for her, I should have begun taking better care of her.

"If Nikel has not addressed her absence from work, that could also pose a problem," Avgust said, finally speaking. "It's a reasonable assumption that her work might conduct a welfare check, depending on her attendance record."

"A part of me wishes that they'd get involved, but I am also very aware that we do not need the police muddying up the waters more," I replied, drowning in the irony that my intelligence level was useless in this situation.

Just then, my phone chimed with an incoming text, and when I looked at my phone, I saw that it was an attachment, and I'd never felt such an overwhelming sense of dread in all my life. Even when I'd been fifteen and put in charge of raising Akim.

"It's an attachment," I said, my fingers hovering over the screen.

"Do you want me to look at it first?" Avgust offered, knowing exactly what I must be feeling, having been here before.

"No," I answered.

Two seconds later, I opened the attachment, and regret almost dropped me to my knees as I watched Nikel tell Katja to smile for the cameras. She was about to be violated for an audience again, and it didn't matter that it was just an audience of one. Once again, all of Katja's secrets were going to be exposed for entertainment purposes, and I knew in this moment that I was never going to be able to make things right between us. Yeah, I had the power to keep her with me forever, but she was never going to love me, and that was as clear as day now.

I watched the video, not saying anything as Nikel cut her bra open, showing the camera everything, his hands touching her like they had the right to. I watched as she kept her head down, her eyes glued to her lap, Nikel's face glowing with a fevered sickness. Not only was he touching something exquisite, but he also knew what this would do to me. I was never going to get this image out of my head, and I wasn't stupid enough to believe that more videos weren't going to follow.

When the video finally ended, I looked over at Avgust, and he must have seen something in my eyes, because he immediately stood up, asking, "What is it?"

"It's a video of him and Katja," I answered, not needing to go into details.

Very calmly, he said, "I need you to look at it again, Maksim. However, this time, I need you to ignore Nikel and Katja, and look at anything in the background that can tell us where they are."

I gave him a terse nod before doing as he'd instructed. Pulling up the video again, I did my best to ignore the atrocity happening in the center of the room. "It's an abandoned house, looks small."

"Like where Louie took Samara?" he asked.

I nodded. "Yeah…in fact, if we hadn't burned down the house, I'd think that it was the same place."

Before Avgust or I could try to connect the dots, Avgust's phone was ringing, and as soon as I saw him put it on speaker, I knew that it had to be Sartori or Morocco. I also knew that if they were calling, instead of sending a text, then this was a lot more complicated than they made it look in the movies.

"Kotov here," Avgust answered.

"I found her," Morocco announced, and I could feel myself shaking with the news.

"Where is she?" I asked.

"Coincidentally, when you guys burned down the evidence of Mrs. Kotov's kidnapping, you missed a deeper hunting cabin just to the left of the main house. It's covered by weeds as tall as the house, and you missed it because the weeds blend in with the trees, obscuring the path to the cabin."

"I am not sure that I know what you are speaking about," Avgust replied coolly.

Morocco snorted. "Oh, please. In the event that you guys weren't able to get a handle on Nikel Ovchinnikov, I've been monitoring any weird shit that's happened since Louie Manziel got stupid, and a random fire in the middle of no-fucking-where was rather weird, Kotov."

*He had a point.*

"Is the front road the only access to the cabin?" I asked, not caring if the Sartoris knew our secrets or not.

"Yes," he answered. "There's no other way in unless you guys want to hike your way in."

"I suggest that you take your best sniper with you," Nero remarked, finally speaking. "It might be the only chance that you have to get her out of there alive."

"There's a creek to the right of the cabin, a quarter of a mile behind," Morocco added. "The sound of water might help you guys sneak in undetected, but that depends on how much water is in the creek and if it's flowing steadily."

"Okay, thanks."

"Good luck, gentlemen," Nero said before adding, "Mrs. Sartori sends her regards."

I let out a hollow laugh, knowing exactly what that meant. At this point, it looked like every syndicate leader owed Mrs. Sartori their lives, and she was proving to be much more cunning and diabolical than her husband. On the outside looking in, a person might assume that she was just being sentimental and a romantic at heart, but that's not what this was. She'd been collecting us like unsuspecting pawns, and we were all going to owe her if the time ever came when she wanted or needed to collect. If Kasen Sartori ended up running the entire state of Maryland one day, I wouldn't be surprised.

"Let's go," I said as soon as Avgust slipped his phone back in his pocket.

"You go," he ordered. "I'll call Damir, Ivan, and Orlyn to have them meet us there. I'll give them the details as you make your way over."

Without another word, I rushed out of my house, got into my car, then raced down the street. Now that I knew where they were, it was nothing to trade my life for Katja's. While I didn't think that it would come to that, I'd do it if necessary. Right now, the priority was getting to her before Nikel could violate her any further. Though this was going to take some time to heal from, every second wasted had the potential to make matters worse, and saving her was all that I could think about.

I also knew that it was a good twenty-minute drive out there, and twenty minutes felt like twenty hours right now. Katja was helplessly tied to a chair, and the first thing that I was going to do when I got her back was teach her some effective self-defense, and none of that local gym crap. I was going to teach her how to kill with her bare hands, something that every woman should know.

As I sped down the street, there was also the issue of what I'd done to her at Millie's. Having always planned on telling her the truth, I knew that the truth wasn't going to matter after it was all said and done. Katja had every right to feel violated because that's exactly what I'd done to her; I had violated her.

Nevertheless, that wasn't going to stop me from making her mine and trying to make it up to her. I was not going to allow one error in judgement to define the rest of our lives, no matter how huge that error. I loved Katja, that fact as clear as any blue sky.

Now I just had to prove it to her.

# CHAPTER 34

*Katja ~*

"Okay, time for another show, *milaya devushka,*" Klive announced, a wicked gleam appearing in his eyes. "This time, you are going to be a good girl and suck my dick like it is your favorite meal of the day."

"You can't make me do that," I said, goading him into doing just that.

"Oh, but I can," he taunted. "A gun to your head will do just nicely, I think."

My heart started racing inside my chest again. I hadn't counted on him holding a gun to my head throughout the ordeal. While I had no other plan in place, he could easily accidently pull the trigger through is pain, but what choice did I have? Sure, I could just let it happen to buy me some more time to come up with a better plan, but the very idea of letting him violate me again was enough to make me throw up. As disgusted as I'd felt with him just touching me, I knew that there was no way that I'd be able to get through having him in my mouth.

I did my best to steady my breathing as Klive stopped to stand in front of me, the fingers on one hand already working to free himself while his other hand pulled the gun from the back of his waistband. He really was going to hold a gun to my head, and what happened next was going to be in God's hands, and I'd never felt the power of hope as I did in this moment.

"Now, you are going to show me exactly why Maksim is so enamored of you, and if you think that I will not put a bullet in your head, then you are very mistaken, *milaya devushka.*"

"Don't do this," I begged, even though I knew that my pleas were falling on deaf ears. "This isn't my fight. Don't do this to me."

"Oh, but it *is* your fight," he replied condescendingly. "Had you been a better whore, then maybe you would have had something to bring back to me. However, since you could not get Maksim to share his secrets fast enough…well, here we are."

"You can get Maksim another way," I said, trying to stall. "You don't need to do this to me."

Klive slid his free hand behind my head as he pushed the barrel of the gun against my left temple. "But I *want* to do this, *milaya devushka*. You keep going on and on as if you are not a beautiful woman that any man would want to experience. Your tits alone are worth the headache."

As his dick pulsed violently in front of my face, panic and helplessness threatened to take me under again. So many things could go wrong, and it was hard not to lose my mind with the endless possibilities. Since my hands were tied behind my back, I needed to bite him hard enough to incapacitate him. I needed to bite him hard enough that the pain would make it hard for him to function, let alone aim the gun and shoot me with it. I mean, I knew that a man's balls were exceptionally sensitive, but I had no idea if that same sensitivity extended to their dicks.

Then there was what to do after I bit him. Did I take off running the best that I could? Did I try to break free from the chair? Since my legs weren't tied down, then running would be my best option, but I had no idea how far I'd get with the chair hindering me the way that it would. Of course, I could use it to block any wayward spray of bullets, but all of that really depended on how badly I hurt him. Though the thought was revolting, I knew that biting him was my only chance at getting away.

"Now, while you might not love me, I want you to pretend that you do," he went on. "I want you looking up at me with those wild eyes of yours and make me believe that I am the man of your fucking dreams, *milaya devushka.*"

"Don't do this," I begged one last time. "Please… don't do this."

"Open up, Katja," he instructed as he tapped the side of my head with the gun. "Show me why Maksim kept you around."

With all the oxygen in my lungs trapped by fear of failure, I opened my mouth as wide as I could, then as soon as Klive slid his dick into my mouth, I waited until he was halfway in before I turned my head, then bit down on him as hard as I could with my back teeth.

His howl shook the single-pane windows, and just as I felt blood coating my tongue, I felt his hand grab a chunk of my hair to try to pull me off of him. When I finally opened my mouth to set him free, Klive fell to the floor, his screams rattling my eardrums.

"You fucking bitch!" he screamed. "I'm going to kill you!"

I watched him raise the gun, and I dropped to the floor just in time to miss the shot that rang throughout the room. When I landed hard on the rotted wood, the chair splintered apart underneath me, and then I scrambled to get to my feet. However, before I could make a run for it, pain was a livewire as it shot up my left leg.

I immediately fell back onto the floor, and it didn't take a genius to realize that I'd been shot. Panicked beyond all reason, instead of making another run for it, I rolled over until I was lying next to Klive, and with all the strength that I possessed, I kicked my leg out, hitting him in the groin, the shot to his balls making him cry out in agony, and I didn't stop until blood was spraying everywhere.

As he dropped the gun to cup himself, trying to ease the excruciating pain, I scrambled over his body, and though my hands were still tied behind my back, splinters of wood still hanging from the ropes, that didn't stop me from trying to pick up the gun. I fought and fought with trying to grip the handle, and when Klive noticed what I was doing, he tried to stop me, grabbing my thigh and making me cry out in pain myself.

Aiming for anything that I could, I threw my head back, and then white stars danced behind my eyes as I made contact with Klive's skull, and the pain almost threatened to make me black out. However, as he swore a blue streak, I rolled over, then began kicking him in his groin again, and fresh blood bathed my jeans as I kicked with all my might.

The second that Klive reached down to cover himself again, I went back to trying to get a hold of his gun, and when I finally succeeded, I started pulling the trigger wildly, bullets hitting the walls, shattering the windows, and ricocheting all over the living room. It wasn't until I heard muffled cries that I turned around to see two bullet holes in Klive's chest.

I immediately dropped the gun, then collapsed on the floor, my leg burning with the fire of a thousand suns, my shoulders feeling like they were about to pop out of their sockets. I knew that the smart thing to do would be to keep shooting Klive until the gun was empty, but now that I was down, I didn't know if I'd be able to get back up. My leg was bleeding badly, and it'd be just my luck that he would have hit an artery.

As Klive laid on the ground, struggling to take his final breaths, I looked around for the knife. I needed to free my hands, then call the police. I no longer cared about the complications, either. I should have called them a long time ago, and so I was doing that now. However, because I had a stupid smart phone, I needed to unlock it, then do all kinds of other shit for the keypad to come up, and I couldn't do that without eyes in the back of my head.

When I finally spotted the knife, I did my best to ignore the pain, then used my legs to push me towards the edge of the couch. It must have fallen off the coffee table during our scuffle, but I honestly didn't care how it'd gotten there. I just needed to cut my binds while also not slitting my wrists in the process. While this was definitely not a time to joke, this shit wasn't like in the movies.

As soon as I reached the couch, I had to stop to take a deep breath. I was already feeling woozy, and it didn't take a rocket scientist to see that as a bad sign. If I passed out now, then I'd die for sure. I needed to free my hands, call the police, then use whatever I could to stop my leg from bleeding out. It also didn't help that my heart was beating a mile a minute, pumping my blood frantically.

Reaching for the knife, I did my best to grab the handle, praying that Klive really was too busy dying on the floor to come after me again. Though that sounded callous as hell, I wasn't immune to the fact that I had just killed another human being. That was something that I was going to have to process later, and it was more than likely going to take some time to move on from it if I was even able. While I was a firm believer in self-defense, killing another person was still something that I couldn't take lightly.

Doing my best to cut through the ropes, my palms were sweaty, so screw the goddamn movies. When the knife slipped out of my hands, I let out a frustrated cry when the fingers on my left hand found the blade, adding blood to the sweat, and just really trying to force me to give up. Luckily, I was made of sterner stuff, so I let out a calming breath, wiped my hands against the fabric of the dirty couch, then tried to pick up the knife more carefully this time around.

*Thank you, God.*

With a lot more finesse than the first time, I concentrated on the movements of the knife, doing my best to work smarter not harder. Though my fingers were stinging from the sweat, I was still able to keep my grip on the knife handle, and while it felt like forever, it was only a few minutes as I was making progress.

As soon as the rope fell free, I dropped the knife, and tears of gratefulness stung the back of my eyes. Now I could call the police and get some help, and whatever happened after that, I'd deal with it when the time came.

However, when I heard the front door of the cabin open, hope drained from my soul, it never occurring to me that Klive might have had a partner.

# CHAPTER 35

*Maksim ~*

With no regard for the law or other people on the road, I'd made it to the cabin in record time, not caring about anything but getting to Katja before it was too late. I also hadn't cared about waiting for the others. If Nikel wanted my life for Katja's, then I was fine with that. If I could get the both of us out of here alive, then great. However, if I couldn't, then it wasn't the hardship that Nikel thought it might be. I was in love for the first time in my life, and now I understood why Avgust had been a miserable sonofabitch after Samara had left him all those years ago. Men didn't love easily, but when we did, it was no joke.

With the help of the satellite picture that Morocco had sent to us, I'd been able to access the creek, then make my way on foot towards the cabin. While he'd been right about the waters not rushing fast enough to cause a lot of noise, it'd been running fast enough to camouflage footsteps. So, after texting Avgust, Damir, Ivan, and Orlyn where I was parked and how I'd made my way down the creek, I'd been able to make it to the cabin undetected.

However, once I'd gotten close enough to see through one of the dirty kitchen windows, I hadn't expected to see Nikel Ovchinnikov lying dead in the center of the living room. When I couldn't see deep enough inside the room to see where Katja was, I made the decision to just go inside. If she wasn't here, then I could see if Morocco could get live satellite feeds to see if she was still in the area, but not before I searched every fucking inch of the cabin. Still, because I wasn't stupid, I walked around the structure, peeking into every visible window that I could find, and it wasn't until I looked into the living room window that I saw Katja sitting on the floor, and while she was leaning back against the couch, it was very clear that Nikel was dead.

After firing off another text that the cabin was clear, I wasted no more time in opening the front door. Ignoring the dead body of my blood, I raced over to Katja, then dropped on my knees in front of her, and that's when I noticed that the lower half of her face was covered in blood. "Baby."

She opened her sunshine-colored eyes, and looking into my worried face, she said, "I'm pretty sure that I'm dying."

At that, my eyes raced over her body, and that's when I saw the blood flowing out of her left leg. I quickly pulled my shirt off, then ripped it to shreds, tying a tourniquet around her thigh. As soon as I was finished with that, I re-fastened her shirt, covering up her bare chest. My heart was beating wildly in my throat, and I could barely speak with how damaged she looked.

"Are you shot or hurt anywhere else, *lyublyu?*"

She held up her left hand. "I cut my fingers."

Taking an extra strip of my shirt, I wrapped her fingers, my hands shaking with regret at not being able to kill Nikel myself. "Anywhere else?"

Katja shook her head. "No."

Just then, I heard footsteps entering the cabin, and when I turned my head to see who it was, Avgust was walking in, and when he saw me on my knees, he jerked his head to let me know that the others were behind him. So, getting to my feet, I reached down, then picked Katja up bride-style just as the others entered the room.

As soon as I saw Orlyn, I said, "She's been shot in her left leg, and her fingers are also sliced."

"How long do you think you've been bleeding," he asked her as I laid her on the dirty couch.

"I don't know," she answered tiredly. "A while."

Orlyn shot a look my way. "We cannot wait for an ambulance."

"And a hospital will ask too many questions," Ivan added.

Not caring what I had to do to save this woman, I pulled my phone out, then dialed my enemy like we were all one happy family. Still, I hadn't been lying when I'd said that I would give my life for Katja.

"Barychev, what an unpleasant surprise," Noah Murphy drawled out like an ass.

"Does your brother still occupy the cabin that he saved Samara in?"

"Why?" he asked, though the tone in his voice had changed drastically.

"My girl just killed Nikel Ovchinnikov, but he was able to shoot her in the process," I told him. "We're in a back cabin near the creek where we found Louie. Name your price, and I'll pay it. Even if it's my life."

"I'll call Lochlan now," he said. "Come alone, Barychev. If Kotov is with you, then that's fine. I'll let The O'Brien know."

As soon as I hung up, I said, "We're welcomed, but only me and Avgust."

"You guys go," Damir said. "We'll take care of the mess here."

"He...he said that he picked me because...because Samara and her sister were too well guarded," Katja said, surprising us all. "He...he also said that Maksim was the easier target since Akim was with his family all the time, and they were also all very well guard...guarded."

"Get her to the O'Briens, Maksim," Orlyn instructed. "And do not let her pass out before then."

"I'll drive," Avgust announced, and trusting the others to do what they did best, I carried Katja to Avgust's car.

I held her in my arms as Avgust drove, and with my heart still pounding in my chest, I said, "Look at me, *lyublyu.*" Katja opened her eyes, her gaze looking dim and vacant. "We're getting married, Katja."

Her head jerked a bit. "Wh…what?"

"We're getting married," I repeated. "We're getting married, and because you'll be my wife, you'll have to quit your job."

Her eyes narrowed at me, and that's what I wanted. I wanted to keep her awake like Orlyn had instructed, and I knew that anger was the only way to do that. I needed her fired up and mad enough to have this argument with me.

"I am…am not marrying you," she said, her voice sounding stronger. "You're…you're out of your mind if…if you think that…that I'm going to marry you."

"Oh, but you are, baby," I informed her. "I have already emptied a room for your dedushka, and as soon as you are well, we can start interviewing real nurses for his care since he will be well guarded at the house."

"You…you…you can't do that," she sputtered. "You can't just…just take us like…like you're adopting an animal from the shelter."

"Baby, I love you," I finally told her. "Maybe not in the way that you deserve, but I still love you, Katja."

She started shaking her head. "That's not fair. You…you can't just say…say that to me."

"Why not? It is true."

"It's not…not true," she argued. "I don't…don't know why you're saying it, but…but it's not true."

"It is," I insisted. "It is, and I just need you to let me prove it to you."

Fire flared in her eyes, and she didn't care that Avgust could hear her when she spat, "How? By fucking me…me in a room full of people without my knowledge again?"

"As soon as we get home, I will explain that situation to you," I promised her.

"Is your…your explanation going to undo it?" she asked, and my heart stopped beating when she closed her eyes, then let out a shuttered breath.

"Avgust?"

"We're almost there," he assured me, speeding as fast as he could without killing all three of us.

"Katja, I need you to look at me," I told her. "I need you to keep your eyes open."

"Why? So that you can keep…keep fighting with me?"

"So that I don't lose you, baby," I said, the words feeling like they were stuck in my throat. "I need you to keep looking at me so that I do not lose you."

Katja let out a hollow laugh. "Joke's on you, Maksim. I wasn't lying when I said that I was pretty sure that I was dying. You just have to look at my blood-soaked jeans to know it."

"You can lose up to thirty percent of your body's blood before things begin to get serious," I told her. "We are going to get you help before it gets beyond that."

"Because the O'Briens are really going to help me?" she scoffed. "Highly unlikely."

Because no one knew about our unspoken truce or the fact that Kasen Sartori was an evil mastermind, I could see why Katja would be hesitant to believe that the O'Briens would help us. If she wasn't weak from so much blood loss, then she'd be questioning why I had called them in the first place.

"Katja, you heard me on the phone," I reminded her. "I offered them whatever they wanted."

Her brows furrowed a bit, and I immediately started panicking when she closed her eyes again. However, she opened them back up before I could begin to shake her. "You offered them your life."

I gave her a tight nod. "I did."

"Who serves themselves up to their enemy like that?" she muttered, more to herself than anything else.

"A man in love, baby," I answered.

Before she could say anything to that, Avgust announced, "We are here."

# CHAPTER 36

*Katja ~*

I'd never met either Noah or Lochlan Murphy before, but when Maksim had carried me into a makeshift clinic, I'd been blown away by how blue their eyes were. They were this bright cerulean color, and their dark lashes made them look like they glowed. They were as hypnotizing as any witch's gaze, and when they belonged on faces as gorgeous as theirs, the combination could really throw a girl for a loop.

At any rate, when we'd gotten here, Maksim had immediately placed me on a gurney, and Lochlan Murphy had introduced himself before quickly going to work. Maksim and Avgust had remained by the kitchen area, informing Noah Murphy of everything that had happened, and while this entire situation seemed weird when you considered that these men were supposed to be mortal enemies, I just couldn't summon the energy to care.

After Lochlan was done hooking me up to an IV and a vitals monitor, he looked over at Maksim. "Barychev, I need you." Maksim quickly made his way over, and once he was standing on the other side of the gurney, Lochlan told him, "I can put her out for this part, or you can hold her hand. I'll apply a local if I keep her awake, but digging out a bullet isn't for the weak. This is going to be uncomfortable, no matter the strength of the local."

"Wait...why can't you put me out?" I asked, the imagined future pain making me panic a bit.

Lochlan's face softened. "Because it'll be a long while before you wake up again, especially considering all the blood that you've lost, lass. Kotov and Barychev aren't going to be welcomed here that long, and I can't see Maksim leaving you here with us."

My eyes shot Maksim's way, and he immediately confirmed what Lochlan had said. "I will not leave you here, Katja. You are only here so that Dr. Murphy can provide you with fluids and stop the bleeding until I can get you home. We have our own doctor on call that can see to your aftercare."

I pressed my hand against my stomach, nausea threatening to take over. Even with a local anesthetic, I'd be able to feel Lochlan digging around in my leg, and with the way that I was feeling, was I even guaranteed to live? While that might sound a bit dramatic, I knew nothing about medicine, so I really had no idea how bad off I was.

Looking into Lochlan Murphy's crazy-colored eyes, I asked, "Am I going to die? I mean, is there still a chance that I'll die?"

"Not on my table," he replied confidently. "However, there's always a risk of infection afterwards, lass. This place isn't held to the standards as a sanitized hospital or clinic. This place is to save lives in a pinch, but that's it."

"It's going to hurt, isn't it?" I asked like a scared child. "Even with the local anesthetic, huh?"

Before he could answer, the front door opened, and in walked none other than Declan freakin' O'Brien. Now, while I'd never met him, who else could it be? I couldn't think of anyone else that would just walk in here like that, like they knew that they could. Not to mention that he had that fair Irish look about him, and even with the loss of blood that I had experienced, I could still see that The O'Brien was just as gorgeous as the others in his family. Seriously, what was in the water around here?

Confirming what I was thinking, Maksim said, "That's Declan O'Brien."

"I figured," I muttered as I watched the man shake hands with Avgust before heading my way.

With his blue gaze on Maksim, he said, "Not sure what we keep doing wrong here, but I take it that it's done?"

As he asked the question, Avgust and Noah walked over to join in, and it was a very intimidating thing to have all these powerful men surrounding me. They were all tall, broad, and gorgeous, and it also hadn't escaped my attention that they were enemies. While the underlining tension wasn't as thick as you'd think, it was still there, and I knew that there was no way that Maksim was going to leave me here with them after Lochlan patched me up.

"It's done," Maksim replied, though I wasn't too sure what they were talking about.

Declan looked over at Avgust, then said, "Are you sure that he was the last of them?"

"As far as we know," Avgust replied. "However, even if he was not, I cannot see anyone else picking up his cause since it was a personal one."

Declan nodded. "Agreed."

"The scene is also being taken care of," Avgust assured him.

The O'Brien gave him another quick nod before looking my way. "How are you feeling, lass?"

"Like I've been shot," I muttered.

Declan grinned, and he really was gorgeous. "It's not a fun feeling." Then he looked over at Lochlan. "What are all the injuries?"

"Bullet in the leg, fingers on her left hand were sliced up a bit, but that's the worst of it." Cocking his head in my direction, he asked, "There was blood on your face before I gave you that washcloth, so is there some dental damage or something else that I'm not aware of?"

My face turned beet red. "No...uhm...that's how I got away."

"What do you mean?" Maksim asked.

I looked over at him. "He wanted to...he wanted to make another video of me...of him in my mouth, and so...well, when he put it in my mouth, I bit down and...and that's how I got free."

Every man in the room winced.

"Everything's on my phone," I said, and then that's when I started looking around. "Where's my purse? My phone?"

"The guys have collected your things, and they will be returned to you when we get home," Maksim answered, his voice sounding raspier than before.

"Yeah, so...uhm, if I put her out to extract the bullet, then she'll be out for a while," Lochlan announced, his voice sounding a bit strained. "Barychev isn't too keen on leaving her here with us."

Declan smirked. "Understandable."

"I'm giving her a local," Lochlan went on to explain.

The O'Brien's blue eyes slid Maksim's way. "Are you sure about this?"

He nodded, speaking for me. "She'll be fine."

Returning the nod, Maksim grabbed my right hand, knowing better than to grab my left one. Then, looking me straight in the eye, he lied to me, saying, "It is going to be fine, *lyublyu.*"

"That's easy to say when you're not the one that's getting a bullet extracted from their leg," I retorted, trying to hide just how nervous I really was.

"Awe, lassie," Lochlan drawled out. "I'm pretty certain that every man in this room has had a bullet removed at one time or another." He grinned sweetly at me, his voice back to normal. "I know for a fact that my brother and The O'Brien have."

"If left up ta my wife, I'da had a couple o' mere," Noah Murphy remarked, and holy freakin' hotness on that accent of his.

"You will be fine, Katja," Maksim repeated, his dark gaze narrowing at my newest fascination with the Irish accent. "I would not put you through this if I did not think that you could handle it."

"We'll give you some privacy, lass," Declan added. "Kotov can keep me and Noah company by telling us all what happened."

"Thank you, Mr. O'Brien," I replied quietly.

"I'm going to cut your pant leg off, then I'm going to disinfect the area, give you the local, and after it sets in, I'm going to do my best to extract the bullet," Lochlan said, speaking to me like I might become hysterical at any moment. "Once I remove the bullet, I will sew you up, patch the wound, then send you on your way with some very effective pain medication."

I gave him a tight nod before looking back over at Maksim. "What am I supposed to tell my grandfather?"

"I will handle your *dedushka*, Katja," he promised. "Let us just get this done."

I let out a heavy sigh before looking back at Lochlan Murphy. "I'm...okay, I'm ready."

He let out a soft chuckle before he put on a pair of gloves, then went to cutting off my pant leg right below the tourniquet that Maksim had fashioned for me. When he was done, he slid the fabric down my leg, letting it pool at my ankle. Maksim nor Lochlan spoke as Lochlan did his thing, and even Avgust was keeping his voice down as he told Declan and Noah what had happened. The entire thing felt oddly uncomfortable, but probably because these men weren't supposed to get along. I supposed that was why I was feeling more and more unwelcomed by the second. Though the O'Briens had been nothing but kind to me since we'd gotten here, I still felt like my association with Maksim made me an unpleasant inconvenience.

After Lochlan was satisfied that the local anesthetic had done its thing, Lochlan began to dig into my leg, and I immediately turned towards Maksim, holding onto him like a lifeline. It hurt like a sonofabitch, though still not as badly as I'd expected. However, it still hurt, and after the kind of day that I'd had, I deserved for someone to comfort me, and that someone was going to be Maksim Barychev, even if I was still mad at him.

# CHAPTER 37

*Maksim ~*

As soon as Lochlan Murphy had finished removing the bullet from Katja's leg, I'd gotten her out of there and had brought her to my home. Of course, we had thanked the O'Briens, and after assuring Declan that the situation was over, we had parted ways, hoping to never have to deal with each other again. Granted, we always had business to attend to, but that was a relationship that we were all used to.

At any rate, once we'd gotten to my home, I had taken Katja directly to my room, and though Lochlan had advised against taking her home without an IV to replenish her fluids, he'd given me a list of things to help her recover from the blood loss, and Avgust had also called Dr. Seaport to meet us at my house. Though I'd never had a non-member of the bratva come to my home in the country, Katja was the exception to all my rules.

After Dr. Seaport had checked her over, he had assured me that she'd be fine and that there was a reason why Lochlan Murphy had a reputation for being one of the best doctors in the state. Nonetheless, I still made him look over the aftercare instructions and check Katja out for himself. Once we were all satisfied that she was out of the woods, Dr. Seaport had gone on his way, and I'd made the phone call to the Tremaine Group, informing them that Katja would be submitting her resignation later today, and I had also called Artur to let him know what was going on. Thankfully, no one from Katja's work had called the police or her grandfather to locate her when she hadn't shown up for work.

Dr. Seaport had also taken two vials of her blood, though he really hadn't wanted to. With as much blood as she'd lost, taking more blood hadn't been the wisest thing to do, but since she'd bitten Nikel's dick hard enough to draw blood, it was important that she get tested for any diseases that Nikel could have contracted.

Akim had also been here to greet us when we had arrived, and while Dr.

Seaport had been tending to Katja, Avgust had been telling Akim everything that had happened. Though it was finally all over, the lack of closure was still bothersome. I'd had so many questions for Nikel Ovchinnikov, but given the choice between closure and Katja's life, I was more than glad that she'd been able to save herself. Besides, we already knew most of why he'd come here, so I wasn't sure how much more we would have learned, but still.

"What did The O'Brien mean when he said that he wasn't sure what you guys kept doing wrong?"

I'd just entered the bedroom from walking Akim out, and while I'd been expecting Katja to be asleep from exhaustion, she was sitting up in my bed, Naslediye curled up beside her like she no longer belonged to me. While I should take exception, they both looked perfect lying in my bed together.

Since Katja was going to be my wife, I saw no sense in shielding her from the life that I led. "Nikel came to Port Townsend five years ago, and he immediately started causing problems for all of us, though they were small problems at the time," I told her. "And though unrelated, it seems as if...as if we had not been quick enough to handle matters on our own."

Her brows furrowed over her tired eyes. "What's that mean?"

"The underground world is run differently than the postcards of America that you usually see. Unlike us, people usually delved in gossip for entertainment reasons. However, we keep our ear to the streets because knowing everything about our enemies is vital for survival." Needing to touch her, I finally walked over, then sat on the side of the bed, my hand reaching out to rub her uninjured leg. "Five years ago, Nero Sartori wiped out the Schulz organization because they kidnapped his wife. However, not before Kasen Sartori shot and killed the guy that set her up. A year after that, Savina Provenza was caught up in a murder scandal-"

"I remember that," she quickly rushed out. "It was all over the news. She killed Congressman Oliver's son."

I nodded. "The rumor was that he had been abusive during their courtship, but before Aurelio could take care of it for her, Mrs. Provenza took matters into her own hands and killed him herself. Then, after that, Declan O'Brien met his wife, Keavy, and she is...unconventional to say the least. It is reputed that she has a penchant for killing people, and she is the one that took out most of Nikel's gang."

Katja's eyes widened. "Are you serious?"

I nodded again, still rubbing her good leg. "Then you have Noah Murphy's wife, Shea. Someone tried to kill her, and for someone not of this life, she adapted rather well. She ended up killing two men while trying to save herself, and Noah had not been lying when he'd said that his wife was not above killing him."

Katja shook her head in disbelief. "This is all so...so...wow."

"Then we have Samara Kotov," I went on. "Much like you, she got kidnapped by one of Nikel's associates, and much like you, she had to kill him to save herself. That is how we knew of the cabin that the O'Briens have. Lochlan had patched up Samara after she had managed to kill Louie Manziel."

Katja looked at me for a confused second before saying, "I still don't understand what that has to do with what Declan O'Brien said."

I let out a heavy sigh before telling her the emasculating truth. "As men, it is our duty to protect the women in our lives. For all our money and power in these streets, each one of us has failed to do that. You women have had to save yourselves, and that is a bitter pill to swallow for men like us. When The O'Brien questioned what we kept doing wrong, it was because we keep failing to protect the most important women in our lives."

After a while, she just gave me a quiet nod, her hand reaching out to pet Naslediye. "I can't believe that you have a cat."

"I think it is more that she has me," I admitted. "Cats are very regal, and *Naslediye* is no different."

"What does her name mean?"

"Legacy," I answered. "I named her Legacy."

Though not a surprise, Katja finally said what was really on her mind. "I'm not going to marry you, Maksim."

"I love you, Katja," I told her seriously.

"I don't care," she replied just as seriously.

"You cannot sit there and tell me that you feel nothing for me, Katja," I told her. "I would never believe it."

"That's the thing about people and feelings," she said. "If the feeling is strong enough, you'll allow it to make excuses for you. If the feeling is strong enough, you'll ignore common sense just to achieve the outcome that will make you *feel* better, though not necessarily what is *best* for you. If I only cared about my feelings for you, then this would be easy enough. However, I refuse to be that girl, Maksim."

"Which girl?" I asked, though I was pretty sure which type of female that she was referring to.

"You humiliated me in a way that cannot be undone," she said, her voice sounding a lot stronger than it should be, considering. "Since the moment that I met you, I've been a puppet on your many strings, and that doesn't feel like love, Maksim. In fact, that feels a lot like me just trying to find some light during some of the darkest days of my life, so can I even trust that my feelings for you are real? You manipulated me so expertly that I don't even know what it is that I feel for you."

Doing my best to not disregard her valid feelings and just lay down the law, I said, "You cannot believe that your life can just go back to normal after this, Katja. Even if you could get your job back-"

"What?" she choked out.

"I have already notified your work that you will be submitting your resignation later this evening," I informed her, and I knew that I hadn't done myself any favors when her jaw ticked in annoyance. "Again, you cannot go back to the life that you had before this, Katja."

Stubbornly, she said, "I can move. If my association with you is a problem, then I can move."

"You could," I agreed. "However, do you really think that I will allow that? C'mon, baby."

Instead of facing the truth, she said, "I'm tired, Maksim."

"I will grant you that you need rest, but you cannot avoid this conversation forever, Katja," I said, breaking the news to her. "Sooner or later, we will have to find some middle ground. There is also your grandfather to consider."

She immediately tensed up. "What do you mean?"

"I have already spoken with Artur, and I plan on speaking with your grandfather later this evening about our relationship and what will be expected going forward."

"You're not even listening to me," she practically spat. "What in the hell is wrong with you?"

"I am in love for the first time in my life," I told her. "That is what is wrong with me."

Doing her best to let out a calming breath, if I were a better man, I'd take mercy on her. However, I was in love with someone that didn't love me back, and that made all the difference in the world. While I was confident that Katja cared for me, it was going to take a miracle for her to ever love me, and I knew this.

*I knew this.*

Still, it made no difference.

# CHAPTER 38

*Katja ~*

I wasn't sure what time it was, but when I finally woke up from either a nap or a twenty-four-hour recovery session, I felt worse than I'd had when Klive had shot me. My entire body was sore, and I still felt beyond exhausted.

As I sat up from the bed, I noticed that Maksim's cat hadn't moved an inch, and it still floored me that Maksim Barychev had a cat as a pet. When I thought about men like Maksim, I pictured Rottweilers and Doberman Pinschers as suitable pets for members of the bratva, not a conceited feline.

At any rate, I managed to make my way to the adjoining restroom, and though it took quite an amount of effort, I was able to undress myself, then get into the shower. Granted, there hadn't been much to undress after Maksim had removed my ruined clothing, then had slipped an over-sized t-shirt on me. Of course, that didn't leave me with much to wear after this shower, but I honestly didn't care. My main priority was to get home to my grandfather as quickly as possible. Whether Maksim had spoken to him or not, I knew that he was going to have lots of questions that only I could answer.

After taking my shower, I put my underwear back on, then went in search of a clean shirt and some shorts or sweats. I also didn't care that I might be invading Maksim's privacy by looking through his drawers. At this point, there wasn't a whole lot of consideration that he deserved from me.

Once I was dressed in another t-shirt and a pair of joggers that I'd had to roll up and adjust the waistband, I left the room in search of Maksim. When we had arrived earlier, yesterday, or whenever it'd been, I hadn't had a chance to look around, but now that I was walking around freely, Maksim Barychev had a very nice home. Whatever he did for the bratva, it was very profitable.

When I finally heard some voices breaking through the silence, I headed their way, and that's how I found myself in Maksim's kitchen, and in it were Maksim, Avgust Kotov, and a blonde too beautiful to be real. She looked like she belonged in a Barbie box, her blonde hair falling elegantly around her shoulders, and her blue eyes as bright as crystals. If she was Samara Kotov, then Avgust Kotov was a very lucky man.

As soon as Maksim saw me, he rushed over, his hand reaching for my waist. "What are you doing out of bed, *lyublyu?*"

"I needed a shower, and I'm hungry," I answered tiredly.

"Then you should have called for me," he replied, clearly annoyed with me.

"I was able to manage," I drawled out as he led me to one of the kitchen chairs. "Lochlan did a good job of wrapping my leg and fingers."

"That's beside the point," he bit out.

"I'm hungry, Maksim," I sighed. "If you want to fight, then you're going to have to wait until I've eaten something."

"Why don't you two go get us some Romero's?" the blonde suggested. "I find that I could probably eat a little something myself."

"You are a horrible liar, *Razh,*" Avgust said. "However, if you wish us to leave, we can do that."

The blonde grinned. "I wish you to leave, though I am serious about Romero's. While it's past dinner time, you can grab me an order of pizzelle cookies for dessert."

In absolute amazement, I watched Avgust Kotov walk over to the blonde, kiss her on her forehead, then ask, "What would you like from Romero's, Ms. Volkov?"

"I...uhm, I don't know their menu," I admitted, Romero's way too expensive for my pocketbook.

"Then I will bring back a little of everything," Maksim said. "Whatever you do not like, we can offer to the guards."

"Thank you," I muttered for lack of something better to say. It was obvious that the blonde was in charge, and I didn't know what to make of that.

As soon as Maksim and Avgust left the kitchen-*but not before Maksim kissed me on my temple*-the blonde took a seat across the table from me as she introduced herself. "Hello, I'm Samara Kotov."

"Didn't...didn't Mr. Kotov call you *Razh?*" I asked like an idiot.

She grinned. "It's his nickname for me. It means rage, and he's been calling me that since high school."

My brows shot upward in surprise. "You've been with Avgust Kotov since high school?"

"It's a long story, but I did meet Avgust and Maksim in high school," she answered. "In fact, I've known them all since high school."

Knowing that she sent the men off for a reason, I finally asked, "So, are you going to tell me why you sent the guys to go get dinner when I could have just had a sandwich, Mrs. Kotov?"

She grinned again. "Firstly, please call me Samara. Mrs. Kotov is my mother-in-law, and though I adore her, I'm just not that formal. We get along wonderfully, and as long as she's alive, then she's the one that should be addressed as Mrs. Kotov."

"What do the guards and other people call you when they have to address you?" I asked, slightly curious as to how Avgust Kotov would feel about her casual familiarity.

"They've no choice but to call me Mrs. Kotov, but I really wouldn't care if they called me by my first name," she answered. "In fact, I'd prefer it if they did, but there are some battles that I have to let Avgust win."

"It must be...different to be married to the head of the Russian Bratva," I remarked, feeling wholly unsophisticated.

Her face softened. "You asked why I sent the guys away, and it was so that we'd have a chance to talk. I understand that you're having...well, that you're having some major doubts about Maksim."

I let out a hollow laugh. "I guess I shouldn't be surprised that you know, considering."

"Katja, I know because I'm Avgust's wife," she quickly corrected. "I know because I needed to know everything that was happening with Nikel Ovchinnikov...or Klive Simpson as you knew him to be."

"Why?"

"As the wife of the Pakhan, it's good business for me to know everything," she explained. "If something were to ever happen to Avgust, I'm safest by knowing everything that he knows."

"Okay, that makes sense," I agreed. "However, what's the point of this? Why care what happens between me and Maksim?"

"Because I've been where you are, Katja," she replied candidly. "I know what it's like to be in love with a man that has betrayed everything that you've ever felt for him."

"Oh, Mr. Kotov also had sex with you in front of rooms full of strangers," I deadpanned.

"No," she replied easily, ignoring my sarcasm. "He chained me to a room in one of their torture facilities, then left me there where one of his men tried to rape me."

I could feel shame creep up my spine. Like most people, nothing ever happened until it happened to you, and I'd just fallen into that category. I was acting like worse things didn't happen to other people all the time. I was acting like Maksim had owed me something, and he'd hadn't. I'd been the one that had invaded his life, not the other way around. So, while what he'd done was unforgiveable, I wasn't exactly without blame myself. After all, I had signed up to betray a member of the Russian Bratva, and the repercussions could have been a lot worse.

"If I didn't have feelings for him, this would be so much easier to deal with," I admitted.

"Feelings are the messiest things around," she agreed. "However, I've known Maksim Barychev since I was a teenager, Katja. So, I can tell you that he will never let you go. A man like Maksim doesn't love easily, and I'm pretty sure that Akim and his two nephews are the only other people that he's ever loved."

That had my brow furrowing. "What about his friendship with-"

Samara put her hand up to stop me. "Maksim's relationships with the bratva are about loyalty, Katja. In fact, most everyone's relationships within the organization are about loyalty. That's the foundation upon which the bratva was built upon. Now, while I'm sure that Maksim has some love for Avgust as they've been best friends since before I'd met either of them, loyalty is what keeps him by Avgust's side, not love."

"So, what are you saying?"

Her face softened again. "I'm saying that you need to find a way to work through your feelings of resentment towards Maksim, or else you're just going to end up miserable. Maksim is not going to let you go, and even if he was willing to do so, you'd never be safe."

"I could always move," I told her, repeating the same thing that I'd said to Maksim.

"You could," she quietly agreed. "Or you could stay here, work things out with Maksim, and get the best care possible for your grandfather." She must have noticed the look on my face, because she quickly added, "I'm not trying to manipulate you, Katja. I'm actually trying to help you. If you didn't care about Maksim, then I'd tell you to run and never look back. However, since you do, I'm advising you to save yourself the hell that he's going to bring to your doorstep until you can't take it anymore."

I started laughing until the laughter turned into tears.

# CHAPTER 39

*Maksim ~*

I wasn't sure what had been said between Katja and Samara, but when Avgust and I had returned from getting dinner, it'd been clear that Katja had been crying. However, since neither woman had remarked on it, Avgust and I had been wise enough not to mention it.

After dinner, Avgust and Samara had taken their leave, and that's when I had called Dr. Seaport over to check on Katja. Though it'd only been a few hours, I wasn't going to take any chances with her life, and I'd also made it clear to Dr. Seaport that Katja was his main priority for the time being.

So, now that everyone was gone, and Katja was back in bed, it was time to finish our conversation, though I knew that it was the last thing that she wanted to do. Nevertheless, it needed to be done, and I didn't want to wait any longer. Though she didn't know it, I had sent her grandfather a text from her phone, stating that she had a late work call and for him not to wait up. I had also spoken with Artur, and he had assured me that Mr. Antonov would be asleep before Katja 'got home' tonight. However, I wanted to speak to her grandfather as soon as possible, and it'd be better for all of us if she and I were on the same page when I did it. So, since I planned on speaking with him first thing in the morning, my conversation with Katja could no longer wait.

Assisting Katja into bed, when she was finally comfortable, I sat down next to her, then said, "While I understand that you must be tired, we cannot put this off any longer, Katja."

"Put what off?" she asked stubbornly.

I shot her a look. "Our talk."

"What's to talk about?" she asked flippantly. "You make the rules, and I'm to follow them blindly. I'm not sure what all needs to be discussed about that."

"Katja, you are trying my patience," I warned her.

Her bright eyes flashed before she said, "Fine, Maksim. Then say what you have to say, so that I can get some rest."

I had to let out a calming breath because she *really* was trying my patience. "That night at Millie's had not been meant to humiliate you. At the time, I honestly believed that you would be working for the bratva once we found Nikel, and so I did what we did with most of our newest recruits. However, by that time, I'd already been invested in you, and so I refused to let anyone else showcase you." Katja just stared at me, unimpressed by my explanation so far. "I thought that I was doing you a favor in allowing you something that would help you keep your grandfather at home with you. While I had no problem footing the bill, I had no plans on footing it forever."

Her jaw ticked as tears sprung to her eyes. "You really are a sonofabitch, Maksim."

"When I realized that I'd made a mistake, it'd been too late to go back," I went on, not bothering to disagree with her since it was true that I was a heartless sonofabitch most of the time. "If I had stopped, then you would have been viewed as one of the lower-class options, and things would have just gotten worse for you after that."

Her eyes rounded in disbelief. "Are you seriously sitting there, telling me that you did me a *favor?* Are you serious?"

"No," I answered truthfully. "I'm just explaining what would have happened had I not followed through on why I'd taken you there."

She shook her head at me. "Maksim, no matter what you say, it changes nothing. People saw me at my most vulnerable, believing that I'm a whore for purchase."

"No, they do not," I corrected. "After I realized my error, I spoke with Avgust, and he immediately went into damage control."

"What the hell is that supposed to mean?"

"By then, everyone in the bratva knew that we were looking for Nikel Ovchinnikov," I explained. "He was a top priority, so it was hardly a secret that we were willing to do anything to find him. So, between the bounty on his head, the whispers on the street, and how his entire crew had already been obliterated, Avgust put the word out that you belonged to me, and with that, the show that we put on at Millie's had been to draw Nikel out and nothing more. When the calls for you came in, Melor made it clear that you were not for sale, and that pretty much backed up Avgust's story."

"So?" she asked when I was finally done. "What is any of that supposed to change? You still had sex with me in front of complete strangers without my permission. While some women might look the other way if you flashed enough cash in their faces, I'm not those other women, Maksim."

Katja wasn't going to budge, and I could see that now. Credit to her, she was one of the strong ones. Katja Volkov knew her worth, and no explanation from me was going to make her forget that. I also felt sorry for her because that self-worth of hers was going to make our marriage difficult, though it was fair to say that I probably deserved it.

With that fight one that was never going to be over, I decided to do what I did best, and that was to take control of whatever situation I found myself in. "In speaking with Artur, I found out that there is a lot more to you and your grandfather's living arrangement other than just being family."

Her back straightened. "What do you mean?"

"I learned that the house in which you live is the same house that your grandfather and grandmother lived and raised their family." Those tears were back. "I learned that your grandfather's entire life with his wife is in that house, and that is why it was so important to you that he live with you. It is why you refused to give up the house, despite the financial struggles."

"What's your point?" she bit out, clearly upset that I was touching on such a personal topic.

"As soon as we get your grandfather settled here, I will arrange for the house to be moved," I informed her. "Being who I am, both properties on either side of my home belong to me, as well as the property across the street. If you agree, we can demolish whichever home you choose, then relocate your grandfather's home to the empty lot. If that's still too far away for you, then we can move the house to the backyard, which is certainly large enough to accommodate the move."

"You…you can't just move a house, Maksim," she said, quickly wiping away her tears.

"Actually, you can, *lyublyu*," I replied. "It just takes money and time to make it happen."

Katja shook her head sadly. "You really are a manipulative bastard."

"I am."

Instead of saying anything to that, she said, "I want to go with you when you speak with my grandfather. I don't want him to worry, and you showing up without me will make him worry."

"As long as you understand that nothing you say or do will change my mind about you, Katja," I told her. "So, if this is another attempt to escape me, it will not work."

Her jaw ticked again. "I just want to be there for my grandfather."

Adding more fuel to the fire, I said, "Do not forget to send your resignation letter, *lyublyu*. Since you cannot win, there is no sense in making this harder than it needs to be."

"Harder for who?" she shot back. "As long as you're getting your way, what does it matter if I'm miserable."

"Because I love you," I told her again. "I love you, and whether it seems like it or not, I do not enjoy seeing you unhappy."

She started laughing, and the sound was an empty one. "Yeah…okay."

"We will also be married as soon as your grandfather gives me permission," I added.

"And what makes you think that he'll grant you permission?" she retorted snidely.

"Because your grandfather is not a stupid man, Katja," I answered. "He has lived in this city long enough to know who he is dealing with, and he is smart enough to understand what that all means, even if you still do not."

"Of course, I know what it means to deal with you," she huffed.

"No, you do not, *lyublyu*," I corrected her. "If you did, then you would know better than to argue with me. If you did, then you would be too scared to."

"Or maybe my love for my grandfather outweighs my fear of you," she countered.

"That is also possible," I conceded.

Moving on, she asked, "What did you tell my boss when you called to tell them that I quit?"

"I told them who I was, then explained how it will no longer be possible for my fiancé to continue to work for them," I answered. "Of course, they naturally agreed and said that they would be more than happy to accept your resignation immediately after received."

"Of course," she replied, though her voice had lost its bite.

"Katja-"

"Just stop, Maksim," she ordered. "Just...stop."

After a few tense seconds, I said, "I will grant you some rest tonight, and we will go see your grandfather first thing in the morning.'

"And after that?"

"We begin moving you guys to your new home," I answered honestly.

# CHAPTER 40

*Katja ~*

My grandfather just stared at me, and it was hard not to wither underneath his knowing gaze. It was obvious that I'd done my grandfather a disservice by underestimating his intelligence and astuteness. While he might not have known exactly what was going on, he knew that I'd lied to him, and that felt worse than anything that I'd ever felt before, apart from the deaths of my family.

"I'm sorry, *Dedushka.*"

"You always were such a bad liar, *Beda,*" he sighed. "I knew as you were telling it that the story about new management was a lie. However, it was either be here for you during whatever it was that you were going through, or else go back to Windmill Gates where I'd be of no use to you. So, I chose to remain quiet and wait for you to tell me the truth."

As soon as we'd shown up to the house this morning, my grandfather hadn't seemed shocked to see Maksim Barychev entering the living room behind me. He'd been having breakfast with Artur, and he'd been as polite as could be when he'd invited me and Maksim to sit with him and Artur at the table. Of course, Maksim had declined breakfast, and afraid that I was going to throw up everywhere, I had also chosen not to eat.

Once seated, Maksim began telling my grandfather the absolute truth about these past few weeks, and though he'd been wise enough to leave out the personal stuff, my grandfather was very aware that I had walked in here limping because I'd been shot.

"I wanted to protect you," I told him. "I...I didn't want you to worry. I didn't want you to...you've already had enough tragedy and sadness in your life, so I didn't want to add to it."

He smiled softly at me. "While I can understand why you felt that way, it's much worse to feel helpless when someone you love is going through a hard time and you cannot help them. That is not what we do, Katja. That is not who we are. You and I are family, and it's a very debilitating thing to prevent me from helping you when you needed it most."

Tears immediately started falling down my cheeks. "I didn't mean to make you feel that way, *Dedushka*. I swear."

"I know that, *detishche*," he replied, and calling me child just made me feel worse. "I know you meant well, and I am extremely grateful that you are okay, and that the situation has been taken care of."

"There is more, Mr. Antonov," Maksim said, making my stomach tighten.

"And what is it, Mr. Barychev?" he asked calmly.

"While I understand that it may seem too soon by society standards, I would like to marry Katja, and I would like your permission to do so," he told him, the tone of his voice obvious.

"I know enough to recognize that my answer will not make a difference," my grandfather replied. "So, why ask, Mr. Barychev?"

"Because you are the only person on this planet that Katja loves and respects," he answered him candidly. "So, you deserve the opportunity to consent or object. However, you are correct. No matter your answer, you and Katja will be moving in with me soon, and she and I will be married as soon as her leg heals well enough to make it to the courthouse. I will not lie to you and let you believe otherwise."

"And how does Katja feel about you, Mr. Barychev?"

"She hates me," he answered honestly, and my heart sank to my knees as my secret stayed locked in my chest. "Again, I will not lie to you, Mr. Antonov."

"And you would marry a woman that hates you?" he asked, his brows furrowed in a bit of confusion. "That hardly makes any sense."

"Yes," Maksim replied confidently. "I love Katja enough to bear the weight of that burden."

My grandfather's brows furrowed deeper over his eyes. "And what of children? You would raise children in a household where their mother hates their father?" My grandfather immediately began shaking his head. "I cannot allow that, Mr. Barychev. The most important thing that parents can do for their children is to love one another, and since that is not the case here, I am going to have to refuse your request to marry Katja."

"Of course, I am sorry to hear that," Maksim replied graciously. "However, it changes nothing."

My grandfather looked so heartbroken over Maksim's claim that there was no way that I could let this go on. I'd always said that I'd do anything for my grandfather, and so that meant that I needed to put my pride aside and do the right thing. Unfortunately for me, the right thing at this moment was to tell the absolute truth, no matter the cost to my heart and soul.

"*Dedushka*, I do not hate Maksim," I finally said. "I'm angry with him, and I still have to work through a lot of hurt that I've experienced during these past few weeks, but I don't hate him."

"Then why does he believe that you do?" he asked, refusing to let me hide from this.

"Because he deserves to suffer for what he put me through," I answered, the truth finally breathing some air. "Because he doesn't deserve easy. Because I'm still angry at a lot of things."

My grandfather's face softened. "Which is your right as a woman."

"But I do not hate him," I repeated. "I do not."

"Even so, will he make you happy, Katja?" he asked. "I could not bare it if you were unhappy, *detishche*."

Proving once again that I'd do anything for my grandfather, I said, "He can once I'm no longer angry."

My grandfather smiled, and I could feel my lungs working again. It also helped that I wasn't lying this time. After I had cried all over Samara Kotov yesterday, I had admitted to caring for Maksim way more than any sane woman would, and Samara hadn't judged me, allowing me to finally come to terms with my own stupidity.

Still, the truth was the truth.

Looking back over at Maksim, he said, "Well, that changes things, does it not? Mr. Barychev, you have my permission to marry Katja and make a family with her."

"Well, now that we are to be family, it is Maksim, Mr. Antonov," Maksim allowed graciously.

"And you must call me *Dedushka*," my grandfather told him, tears stinging the back of my eyes again.

I watched as they shook hands, and once they were done, Maksim said, "The plan is to assign you an actual certified healthcare nurse to replace Artur, but Artur will still be your guard. As you know, your lives are about to change now that we are family."

My grandfather gave him an acknowledging nod. "I understand."

"Well, if that will be all, Katja and I have some things that need our attention," Maksim said as he stood up from the table. "We will keep you informed as the plans to move your home develop."

"I'm sorry?" my grandfather asked, confused again.

"As I understand the sentimental attachment that you have to your home, we will be moving the entire structure when we move you, Mr. Antonov," Maksim told him. "We will not be leaving your wife behind."

I watched my grandfather's eyes cloud with emotion, and I had to quickly wipe away a couple of tears of my own. No matter what was between me and Maksim, I was always going to be grateful for this moment and the consideration that he was showing my grandfather.

"Thank you," my grandfather replied, emotion clogging up his throat.

At that, I stood up from my seat, then walked around the table to give my grandfather a kiss on his cheek. "I love you, *Dedushka*."

"And I love you, *Beda*," he chuckled.

Neither Maksim nor I said a word as we walked back out towards his car, but the second that Jurik started up the engine, Maksim was reaching for me, pulling me over his lap, careful of my wounds. Once again, he didn't care that Jurik was driving, and I wondered if Jurik was going to be officially assigned to me now that Klive was dead and no longer a threat to Maksim or Akim.

"Once your leg is better, we are going to get married, and I am going to show you all the different ways that I am dying to love you, Katja," he said. "While I cannot undo what has been done, I can guarantee that only memories will ever make you feel like that again. For the rest of my days, I will do everything that I can to be worthy of you, even if you never come to be able to love me. I will accept you not hating me if that is all that you can ever give me."

"I'm just so tired, Maksim," I said, my feelings too jumbled up to know which ones were real and which ones were temporary.

"I know, baby," he said, tucking a wayward strand of hair behind my left ear.

Staring into his dark gaze, I told him the absolute truth of what I wanted, even though I hadn't really known it until my grandfather had mentioned it. "I want my children to grow up seeing me happy, Maksim. I want them to know that happiness is possible, even in the life that they're going to live."

"Tell me what to do, and I will do it, *lyublyu,*" he said. "I will do anything."

Since I wanted to believe him so badly, I chose to, and it finally felt right.

# EPILOGUE

### *Maksim – (One Year Later) ~*
"Oh, God…harder…"

I grabbed my wife by her hips, then slammed into her hard enough to make the desk move. Katja was sprawled out on top of the expensive oak, and her big tits were bouncing beautifully with each thrust of my hips. My hands were gripping the back of her knees as I held her legs spread open for me, and my wife taking my cock was a sight that I was never going to get tired of.

"Like that?" I grunted, giving her what she wanted, though still wondering if it was wise.

"God…yes…" she whimpered. "Maksim, please…"

"I love when you beg for it, baby," I said, my thrust becoming harder as she tightened around me. "Cum for me, Katja."

"Yes, yes, yes…" she chanted as her body let go, her spasms squeezing my cock hard enough to take me over the edge with her.

"Fuck," I groaned as I felt myself explode inside of her, the force of my orgasm pushing the desk farther back. "Fuck, baby…"

After a few moments of just enjoying the satisfying aftermath, I gathered Katja up in my arms, then carried her to the couch. We were both half-dressed, but I didn't care. My wife had been gratified, I was grateful, and most importantly, my wife loved me, which was more than I deserved.

Six months after Katja had moved in with me, she'd finally said those three little words back to me, and determined to hold onto them forever, I'd gotten her pregnant immediately afterwards. So, with her grandfather living across the street from us, his health well, Katja loving me back and being pregnant with my child, I wanted for nothing in this world, and there wasn't anything that I wouldn't do to keep this feeling forever.

"We are going to have to let up soon," I warned her as she rested comfortably in my arms. "You are only five-months pregnant right now, but I think once you hit the six-month mark, no more rough sex for you."

She let out a soft laugh. "Way to kill the romance."

"I mean it, Katja. I will not have anything happen to you or the baby," I told her seriously.

"How about we consult with the doctor, then go from there?" she suggested.

"As long as he agrees with me, then fine," I countered.

After a few moments of listening to my wife's steady breathing, I contemplated just allowing us both to fall asleep on the couch, but I could admit that I'd become a bit of a mother hen ever since we found out that she was pregnant. I was over-obsessed about her comfort, and even though I knew that it drove her crazy, I couldn't help myself. With Nikel no longer in the picture, life was back to normal, and I refused to let anything disrupt what I had with Katja.

"I love you, *lyublyu.*"

Tiredly, she said, "I love you, too."

"But I am going to love you forever," I pointed out.

"I know, Maksim."

That was the one thing that she never promised back, and I respected her for it. Though a year was a long time, it really wasn't when you were still processing everything that you'd been through and how you still felt about one of the darkest times in your life. Nevertheless, when she was finally ready to say it back, I was going to be here to embrace the miracle.

"As much as I'd love to stay here on the couch all evening, we promised *Dedushka* that we'd walk him over for dinner tonight," I reminded her. "We should probably shower, so that we will be presentable."

"My protruding belly kind of gives away the fact that we have sex, Maksim," she smirked, and I adored this version of my wife. Now, while I loved all versions of her, Katja being comfortable around me was what I cherished the most.

"While that is true, the poor man doesn't need to smell it on us," I retorted.

"I think you're just trying to get me naked in the shower with you," she teased.

"That I am, *lyublyu.*"

"Well, you should have just said so, Mr. Barychev."

"I'll remember that for next time, Mrs. Barychev."

The End.

# PLAYLIST

I'm In It For Love – James House
Stay – Rihanna ft. Mikky Ekko
Bother – Stone Sour
The Flame – Cheap Trick
Hold Tight – Lvly ft Jaslyn Edgar
Bad Friends – Mimmi Bangoura
Poison – Alice Cooper
Say Goodbye – Jordan Knight ft. Deborah Gibson
Piano in the Dark – Brenda Russell
Habits (Stay High) – Tove Lo

# ABOUT THE AUTHOR

M.E. Clayton works full-time and writes as a hobby only. She is an avid reader, and with much self-doubt but more positive feedback and encouragement from her friends and family, she took a chance at writing, and the Seven Deadly Sins Series was born. Writing is a hobby she is now very passionate about. When she's not working, writing, or reading, she is spending time with her family or friends. If you care to learn more, you can read about her by visiting the following:

Smashwords Interview

Bookbub Author Page

Goodreads Author Page

# OTHER BOOKS

## *Duets & Series*

The Enemy Duet
The Seven Deadly Sins Series
The Enemy Series
Resurrecting the Enemy (Enemy NG Standalone)
The Enemy Next Generation (1) Series
The Enemy Next Generation (2) Series
Embracing the Enemy (Enemy NG Standalone)
The Buchanan Brothers Series
The How to: Modern-Day Woman's Guide Series
The Heavier…Series
The Holy Trinity Series
The Holy Trinity Duet
The Vatican (Holy Trinity NG Standalone)
The Holy Trinity Next Generation (1) Series
The Holy Trinity Next Generation (2) Series
The Eastwood Series
The Blackstone Prep Academy Duet
The Problem Series
The Pieces Series
The Rýkr Duet
The Order of The Cronus Series
The Canvas Duet
When The Series
Expectations Series
The Carmel Springs Series: The Colters
The Carmel Springs Series: The Campions
The Syndicate Duets
The Sports Quintet Series
The Storm Series
The Weight Series
The Through Duet

## *Standalones*

Unintentional
Purgatory, Inc.
My Big, Huge Mistake
An Unexpected Life
Real Shadows
You Again
Merry Christmas to Me
Dealing with the Devil
The Loudest Love
Kimmy & The World of Dating

M.E. CLAYTON

The Right Price
Work Benefits
The Reading
Noctis
Unusual Noises
Murder or Margaritas
Tell Me Your Truths
All of My Life
A Different Kind of Hooker
It's Never *Not* Been You

168

Made in the USA
Columbia, SC
14 December 2024

47920356R00098